TIME'S UP

TIME'S UP

NICK CONNOR

BROWN DOG BOOKS

Published under licence by Brown Dog Books and
The Self-Publishing Partnership Ltd, 10b Greenway Farm, Bath Rd, Wick,
nr. Bath BS30 5RL

www.selfpublishingpartnership.co.uk

ISBN printed book: 978-1-83952-312-0
ISBN e-book: 978-1-83952-313-7

Cover design by Kevin Rylands
Internal design by Andrew Easton

Printed and bound in the UK

This book is printed on FSC certified paper

DEDICATION

I dedicate this to my truly amazing mother
Shirley Eileen Connor (Sharp)
I will forever love, cherish and miss you,
You will always be in my heart.
May 7th 1936–March 18th 2020
Never to be forgotten!

xx

CHAPTER 1

LATE 1990S

Deep in a leafy suburban village on the outskirts of Guildford was a stately mansion set in acres of land. A flickering light in a top window could be seen; the TV shone, and the change of scene or picture was the cause of the flashing light. It was getting late, approaching 10.30, and the BBC news had just finished. The weather was awful, a constant barrage of rain beating down on the window and the odd rustling of trees as the wind blew inconsistently.

Inside a large room sat two men in their late fifties. Patrick turned to Myles. They had just heard the official announcement that the IRA were laying down their arms and would no longer use terrorism as a mechanism of voice; they would campaign legitimately for what they believed in. On the whole, it was a welcome response and a massive cue to seal this agreement for the Labour government and rubber-stamp the leadership qualities of Tony Blair. It was later to be known as the Good Friday Agreement. They stared at each other momentarily, then a grin started to form on Myles' face. He had a plan; he knew Patrick's next words, or at least the gist of them.

Myles' family already had a reputation in the UK for violence and intimidation, a few jobs and hits in the criminal underworld. People knew not to mess but they never stepped the game up in the area as their focus was political direction towards legitimate English targets for the cause. The police were aware of the gang and some jobs they were believed to have done, and a special task force was trying to bring them down, but to date they had no substantial leads. Just hearsay and rumours.

"Now what the hell are we gonna do?" Patrick demanded in a concerned way.

Patrick was a cousin of Myles' and had memories of Bloody Sunday so had no care for the English and would lose no sleep over intimidating and racketeering on the English shores. He saw innocent brothers shot that infamous day and didn't forget.

Myles paused, looked around the room, then glanced back with a smirk and caught Patrick's gaze. Patrick had a scar across his right eyebrow, a constant reminder of his terrorist days; a bit of shrapnel from a stray bullet and, worst of all, from his own man. They call that *friendly fire. What's so friendly about that?* Myles often thought. Needless to say, the soldier in question had a lot to answer for and was squeezed out of the mainland operations the IRA were doing at that time. Those days were long gone and for the better, Patrick often thought. It was a pointless war, deep down, that no one could ever win, and the only losers were mothers on both sides burying their sons.

"We're gonna make even more fucking money! We've got the infrastructure, set-up, manpower, the finance, the contacts, the experience to intimidate these English bastards. They're gonna pay us back in other ways; financially, I mean. We just need to step up our activities," Myles said in a controlled and reassuring way in answer to Patricks question.

"You know what I want done. As from tomorrow, I want you to push the buttons; tell the other units they are to become self-sufficient divisions. I want fortnightly reports, proposal jobs they're working on. No job gets signed off without my say-so though. I sanction all jobs, all hits. That is a must! No private jobs, no skimming for themselves. I've got lawyers, finance people in place, linguistics, any relevant person I can provide for them. I've got people in the police, judges, local councillors and journalists all reporting to me or at my beck and call. They only have to say what they need for a job and I will get it. No cock-ups and no links or trail back to them or me, you understand?"

"Dad, you wanna drink?" Eileen called from behind the door. She knew not to enter when Dad was doing business, best she did not know some stuff. She longed for her dad's attention, but he spent most of his spare time with his sons. Eileen was spoilt from a money perspective and Myles would do anything for her, but something was missing from her point of view. She wanted love and affection, and to be the centre of attention.

"Just a whiskey, love, with ice. You and ya ma OK?" Myles answered back, going through the motions in regard to how they were.

"Is Conor in there with you?" Eileen asked, fully expecting a yes.

"Yes, he's on the computer!" Myles said, a bit annoyed. Myles was getting exasperated with Conor always on the computer.

"Conor, you want anything?" Eileen said, poking her head into the room.

"Ei-Ei-Eileen, I'll have a glass of milk. p-p-please," Conor answered in a stuttered manner.

Now Conor was a whizz-kid with computers and occasionally would hack in to get info for some of the family jobs. In his late teens he was the good-looking one of the family but was also dyslexic a bit, so lacked confidence talking to anyone.

Eileen was Myles' only daughter and he treated her like a princess. Like many father-daughter relationships he worshipped his girl, and would keep her safe no matter what he would need to do; that was his duty today, the next day and always. When Eileen was growing up and going through her doll-princess phase he had an artist come in and paint a magical fairyland mural on all the walls of her bedroom, including a tower with a princess at the top. Added to that were pictures on the walls of scenes from Walt Disney films like the Seven Dwarfs skipping to work on a bridge over a river and, probably her favourite film at the time (*Pinocchio*), the scene of Geppetto carving out the puppet and attaching strings. He always did and got whatever she wanted; she was spoilt to the highest level, but most dads have that doting nature and especially as she was their first and only girl. There was a special bond between father and daughter; unconditional love and pursuit for total happiness for her.

Eileen, nineteen, was the middle of three children; Seamus

the eldest at twenty-five, and Conor the youngest at just eighteen. The family business had kept them to themselves and they were reclusive in a lot of ways, only mixing and socialising with immediate family and a handful of friends. The Irish had a way of keeping themselves to themselves and looking out for one another. Myles had close ties and links to a few other Irish families that now resided in the UK, brought about from his involvement and running of the most feared and ruthless divisions of the Irish Republican Army. Despite his heavy involvement in planned raids and executions during the conflict with the British government, he was never indicted for any single activity. He had been on MI5's radar, but he could never be linked and during the last few years of the struggle he had been very remote, knowing this day would finally come. He had been an unofficial "godfather" in Belfast and the surrounding areas for the past fifteen to twenty years.

The only other person high up in his firm was outside the Irish clan and that was Jack in London; now Jack had great connections and was notorious in the London underworld. He dealt with a lot, as a lot of business was conducted on the streets of London. Myles trusted him implicitly and gave important jobs for him to organise and carry out with his crew.

Eileen went down to the kitchen where her mum was doing some traditional Irish cooking, a kind of stew. The ingredients only the selected few knew, passed down from generation to generation, with the odd tweak made from one mother to another.

"Dad wants a JD and coke. I think I'll do him a double, save my legs later in the evening." Nearly forgetting, she went on,

"Oh, and Conor wants a glass of milk. Mum, Dad's only ever got time for the boys or business, I never have quality time with him," Eileen said in a sad voice.

"Oh, Eileen don't take it to heart. He doesn't have time for me either and I'm his fucking wife!" Judith said in a condemned manner, knowing it was too late to change Myles (and god, she had tried).

She went on, "You won't change Myles; he is driven to keeping us safe and would lay down his body and soul in the process, you have to accept that. You've never wanted for nothing and now he is educating you all, and we're not badly off."

It was true what Eileen said though, Myles spent all his time with the boys, drinking, gambling, illegal dog fighting and one of their favourite pastimes: frequenting strip joints.

"Anyway, I'll take his drink up," Eileen muttered in a depressed tone. She was determined to get his attention, whatever it took.

"Dad, your drink. Can I come in?" Eileen called whilst glancing through the crack of the door.

"Yep, Ei, come in." Myles beckoned Eileen in.

Eileen gave Conor his milk then went over with her dad's drink. She stared at him for a few moments, until he looked back. She still idolised her dad and was pleased he protected the family.

Myles put his arms out, enticing Eileen to come forward for a hug. She did, and they embraced; it was more of a bear hug. Myles was a large chap at seventeen stone and six foot two in height. Many beers had gone into the making of his figure.

Eileen held her father for a second, and it seemed like minutes; he smelt good. He was always clean and well-groomed and took great care of his appearance. Eileen was hatching a plan to get her father's attention, but it meant trouble for some unsuspecting person.

Myles loved his daughter very much and would move heaven and earth to protect her and Eileen knew that, knew that only too well, but that was not enough; she longed to be his main focus, but that was never going to happen with the sons, the lads, the boyos. Myles could do all the things that he shouldn't do and foot the blame at their door if his wife disapproved. Which was nearly all the time.

Myles remembered a time when he was going out for a lads' night (well, day and night) and Judith rammed home the words, "Don't let me find out you've been drinking, gambling or womanising or there'll be hell to pay."

Myles replied, "If you want, I'll become a priest; probably have more fun and no nagging!"

Myles had built up a reputation that was feared throughout the immediate family and outside warring gang rivals. Myles and Patrick had grown up in an area where violence was their backdrop; they were destined for this lifestyle borne down from older generations and it was their upbringing. Myles and Patrick were the generals of the firm, with Patrick second in command, then Seamus, Myles' eldest son. Myles, however, was growing more annoyed with Seamus' exploits and shooting his mouth off a little bit too much.

Myles looked at Patrick then turned around and spoke.

"Keep an eye on Seamus, get him to rein it in – keep his mouth shut or one day he will be our downfall!"

The Mafia, Jamaican Yardies, rival English gangs, and the new eastern European gangs knew of him and his family's reputation. It only took one retaliation against a rival gang to further endorse and enhance their reputation and stock even more.

It happened at a boxing match Myles was attending with his cousin, Nial, back in the early nineties. Nial was not part of the family's violent activities of extortion, kidnapping, etc, but just genuinely liked going out for social events with Myles. Myles had connections and could get tickets for big sporting events, and at the time he idolised Nigel Benn for his never-say-die spirit in a boxing match.

Benn had won the bout and, on the way out, Myles and Nial bumped into some Italian folk, *Mafiosi*, including the head man, being Gianluca, who had also been to the match.

"It's Myles, isn't it, the feared Irishman from Shankhill Road. You have me quaking in my boots," the leader of this small Italian group said sarcastically.

"I think we need to bring you down a peg or two. We are the top firm in England now, so you'd better get ready for that," Gianluca announced.

Myles knew the guy and had had some run-ins, only verbals and threats, but overall, their paths had not crossed. At this time the Irish family was gaining a rapid reputation and was infamous as the top gang family in the UK, London and Manchester in particular. In turn this would bring rivals shooting for the title or more of the action.

The numbers were totally one-sided, maybe ten Italians to Myles and Nial.

One of the Italians pushed Nial, then struck him over the head with a blunt instrument; an ashtray.

"Look, we're not out for trouble. Gianluca, isn't it?" enquired Myles, though he knew who it was.

"*Si*, correct, well we are, and we are as you might say in your didicoy language, going to fuck you up!" Gianluca said with a smile, knowing they had Myles outnumbered.

"Gianluca, my friend is not part of my unit; leave it!" Myles shouted at him.

Gianluca briefly turned round and gave the order just by a look for the Italians to lay into both the Irishmen.

A few guys started putting the boot into Nial and blood was dribbling from his mouth; his nose appeared broken or shattered. Nial fell to the ground and the Italians flocked round him, poised for more violence.

Myles' beast within was coming up to the surface, at boiling point.

In an instant he ran forward, thrusting the back of Gianluca's neck in a downward motion and at the very same time bringing his knee up into Gianluca's face. The crack was sickening, almost a dislocation of the jaw. In the next movement he drew a knife from his pocket and cut one of Gianluca's ears off. A pool of blood formed and expanded within seconds.

Myles grabbed Gianluca and pulled him towards his face.

"I hope this misunderstanding is closed?" Myles said softly into Gianluca's remaining ear. "I know the acting school your little daughter attends and the coffee shop your wife frequents; do you get my drift?"

He threw Gianluca down to the ground and stared at his gang members with an evil, menacing look. The Italians quickly dispersed and disappeared into the night like a pack of hyenas encountering an angry lion.

The incident got around to other gangs instantly, and Myles was now feared to another level. Gianluca survived and retribution was never sought after.

Myles had sent a message, not intended but that was how it was received.

CHAPTER 2

The road was little more than a dirt track to start with, grass, bushes and trees overhanging, all unattended. In the undergrowth was an abandoned settee that had mould or mildew growing, broken corroded springs coming out in every direction, upside down and it had clearly been there for years. Further along was a beaten-up Cortina that must have been fifteen years plus in age, rusty door windows missing, half in undergrowth, half in a ditch. Further along an old gypsy caravan and some disused petrol cans.

The first impression of the dirt road was squalor, abandonment and general neglect. Then suddenly it transformed unexpectedly; yard by yard, unkempt grass verges changed into neatly trimmed grass and beautiful hedgerows and flowers, daffodils and rosebeds on both sides of the track. It then turned into a smooth, well-kept road. Two CCTV cameras were positioned discreetly, attached to trees on both sides pointing down the track. The road widened for another fifty yards, cherry blossom trees lining both sides, then opened into a round, gravel driveway.

Patrick had designed this appearance deliberately to

avoid detection from unwanted guests and in particular the authorities. It looked unsuspecting of a criminal empire.

Adjacent to the gravel driveway sat a grand mansion with two large statues of lions in front of huge strong doors. It must have been two or three-hundred years old. Patrick had just been out on a reconnaissance mission for Myles. He walked through the entrance, and there was security on the door as always. He proceeded to walk down the corridor, which was decorated with affluent art and paintings from all around the world. A piece from Monet, bought and legit, then an art deco piece on the other side (not so kosher) that was probably on the international stolen wanted list.

The mansion was lavish with opulence and wealth, borne out in antiques, but it still had the odd tacky item, normally from Myles' late-night binge-buying on the internet, for example, a fake teak wood-finish jukebox. Patrick could not help laughing inwardly at some of the purchases.

Over the years the Irish operation had become meticulous, and every area of the business was covered and had been researched to the highest detail.

Patrick walked into the first room on the left, normally a lobby waiting room in the olden days but now converted to a security and surveillance room. There were approximately ten people in there, some state-of-the-art computers, GPS tracking info, and data came into the server from all over the world. Information, analysis of potential targets for business, competition and other gangs' activities; even bugs in potential target headquarters. The operation had informers in the police, other gangs and judges in their pockets. In addition to this they had MPs in parts of the country and top government officials feeding them valuable information.

Patrick paused for a moment to talk to the head of surveillance, Jeffrey Dodds, who was an ex-paratrooper involved in some high MI5 operations from all over the world.

"Jeffrey, your team lost again. Pathetic, heading straight back down, I reckon. Anything to report, feedback from our men on the ground?" Patrick asked, expecting an *It's all OK* reply.

"Paddy, all's well, but I am getting concerned with Seamus' activities and lifestyle. He's sloppy and talks too much, especially when he has a few drinks. He draws unwelcome attention and I'm worried he could jeopardise the outfit," Jeffrey replied.

"Oh, he's only having fun; you were young and free once," Patrick said dismissively.

"Well, I don't like it!" Jeffrey said, firmly and menacingly.

Patrick took it onboard. Although Patrick was higher up in the organisation, Jeffrey was good at his job and someone to take direction from. He could handle himself, running the doors on the roughest pubs from Dublin to Belfast.

Patrick wandered back into the corridor. He was heading up to see Myles; they had some business to run through, figures, takings and upcoming jobs. The next part of the hallway had a different theme of art. It was long, lined with some African art, wild elephant and lion statues in bronze. He peered into another room to check on bits; this was an education centre where some of the young Irish lads in the firm were learning English pronunciation and having elocution lessons. Conor sometimes went in to improve his English accent, even though he struggled to be understood. Seamus and Eileen would be in there a couple of times a week also.

At the end of the corridor was a set of stairs that went up to Myles' office, some bedrooms and a second kitchen. As he climbed the steps, he saw family portraits; pictures of Myles with his daughter and wife, plus one with Myles and Eileen; she must have been just six or seven. The love for her daddy shone through in the painting.

Patrick approached Myles' office and could hear raised voices; it was Myles being shouted at by Eileen. As normal, the background classical music was on. Myles, despite being a cold-hearted murderer, loved his music. He would play one piece repeatedly to the annoyance of his close family; it was from the opera *Madame Butterfly* by Puccini.

"No, no, you said you were taking me shopping Friday! I've seen a nice red dress and a necklace and fallen in love with both!" Eileen shouted piercingly. "Can you come out with me and we can have lunch together?"

"No, I can't! Go with your mam and get it, I've got something important to attend to that I can't avoid," Myles said calmly, trying to tone the conversation down to an acceptable level.

"Oh, what, go fucking drinking with the boys again?" Eileen screamed.

"No – business; that's the end of it. Go, I need to think!" Myles shouted now getting annoyed; he had other things on his mind. Their activity was already being flagged up to police and he had to put better orders in place with other elements of the firm.

Also in the room was Myles' other son, Conor; he was dyslexic and very slightly disabled. This could only be picked up when he walked. Conor smiled at Eileen as she left the room and Eileen ignored him as if he were a nobody. Unfortunately, that was how everyone treated Conor but he didn't mind; he had his own interests, namely computers and gadgets.

Patrick watched Eileen leave the room like a whirlwind, knocking a table over with an expensive lamp on it and barging through the door nearly taking its historical hinges off in the process.

"Don't mind me," Patrick said sarcastically. "What's wrong with her; she got her knickers in a twist?"

Myles stared at Patrick unerringly as he entered the room, not even responding to his last comment.

"The police, the fucking police have got wind of some of our activities. They're watching us. They don't know this place yet but it's only a matter of time – we might have to shut this operation down and move. Make sure that everyone is careful – don't leave any clues or traces of our plans. Brief people; everyone's got to be extra careful," Myles said with an air of concern.

Eileen entered the kitchen in tears, and she embraced her mum.

"He doesn't care, I'm invisible to him, it's just his boys he cares about. I'm sick of it, Mum. I will make him notice me one day, one way or another," she threatened. "He's a pig!"

"He does care; he has a lot of business to attend to – he doesn't mean to ignore you."

CHAPTER 3

Nick Scott was your average adolescent moving into adulthood. Lived for the weekends, did not save any money, blew most of it on nights out, drinking and attempting very poorly to pull the opposite sex. He was a manager of a retail shop and quite proud as he was the youngest one in the region. Something he kept reminding his counterparts, plus his old school friends he went around with.

Because he was a manager and he still lived with his mum, he had a lot of money to squander. He did have one pride and joy and that was his car, a Golf GTI and he was the envy of his friends for a brief period of time before they upgraded their cars and caught him up salary-wise. He had three or four friends: Andy Rosemel, Andrew Letterworth, Steve Lloyd and Wayne Aylett. He and Wayne were quite close at this period of Nick's life and they had a lot in common: they played in the same football team, played snooker and failed dismally at pulling girls.

Being a manager, in Nick's eyes this was status and a grand statement for someone with such young years. However, it did bear stress, anxiety and tension. Nick had had a good patch for a period, being top of the area and receiving accolades from his area manager and head office, but when it was not so good, he did feel the heat come down on him. It was a bit like football – *you're only as good as your last game.* This was very much the case in retail; one week he could smash his target, say 130 per cent, have an excellent conversion rate on selling insurances and the next week it could all be upside down, literally.

He was the manager of a shop in Ruislip and had been there six months and in that period had done really well and earnt a few bonuses. He'd learnt his trade from his old manager in Hemel and one of his principles was never to give money back on major purchases like TVs, washing machines, etc. A product at the time in the early nineties that was an emerging necessity was the camcorder.

Nick had tried to instill this ethos to his staff but today one member of staff, Jo-Anne, was trying his patience. She was younger than the rest and was slow in general on most things. She was prone to mistakes, the worst being on Christmas Eve, selling lots of the bestselling Nintendo Super Mario game. That was the good bit; the bad thing was the boxes were empty so come Christmas Day there were lots of snivelling children and subsequently, come 27th December, the first day open after Christmas, there were a lot of irate customers. Nick took the brunt of this and fortunately for her Jo-Anne was off, but her name was mud for a good week after.

One such week, things were not going so well. Jo-Anne came bursting into the stockroom.

"Nick, there's a few guys outside and they want their money back on a camcorder they bought."

"I told you, we don't do money back, we're not a charity. Just be firm with them and hold your ground," Nick said, hoping that would be the end of it. "What did I say just the other day in staff training: we cannot give money back willy-nilly!" he said firmly, wondering where did the expression "willy-nilly" came from and if he wasn't a bit young to use it – too late, it was said now.

Jo-Anne went away and delivered the bad news. Nick could hear raised voices; this was not going to plan. He was going to have to lay down the law with these guys.

She ran back in looking stressed, and tears started to roll down her cheeks.

"I think it's some of those Charlie's Angels you were talking about the other day; they look real mean and as if they want to hurt someone," Jo-Anne said, shaking.

Despite Nick feeling Jo-Anne could be an easy touch, he was loyal and protective to his staff and would back them to the hilt even if they were wrong in some instances.

"It's Hell's Angels not Charlie's Angels!" Nick whispered under his breath as he made his way out on to the shop floor.

"What?" Jo-Anne said, not really listening. She was worried about what was going to happen in the next two or three minutes.

"They have rituals and initiations. I don't think they will take too kindly being compared to cocky know-it-all American bimbos jumping across a screen," Nick said.

Jo-Anne looked at Nick, totally perplexed; it had sailed right over her head.

Nick walked out on to the shop floor. These bikers were the only ones in the store and he just had Bill and Jo-Anne with him. Jo-Anne was a bundle of nerves and Bill wouldn't say boo to a goose. He walked over to the bikers; because there were no other customers around, they would more than likely start being aggressive.

"Jo, which gentlemen were you talking with?" Nick asked.

"It's this man here" Jo-Anne said nervously.

"Thanks, Jo, I will take it from here," Nick said authoritatively. "Hello, sir, I understand you wish to return your camcorder?" Nick enquired politely, but knowing full well that the conversation would not stay on this level for long.

"Go and get the manager, mate. I don't wish to discuss this with the Saturday lad," said one of the bikers.

"I am the manager, sir, and we don't give money back unless it's faulty. It will have to be examined – this will take about a day," exclaimed Nick, upset with the Saturday boy comment. *How far can I stick to the company's procedures*, he thought.

"So, if I throw it against the fucking wall, it'll be faulty then," the biker said in an irate, aggressive tone.

Nick thought that it wasn't worth the potential aggro and wasn't surprised the conversation was going in the gutter. This was their language, whether they were happy or annoyed, he thought.

"OK, you can have your money back," Nick said begrudgingly. It was not worth getting a slap for his company.

Nick did the relevant paperwork and the bikers left the store. Jo-Anne and Bill said he had done the right thing. Nick was not happy; the camcorder was worth £800 and they had only taken a £1,000 up to that point; a poor day, but at least he still had his teeth.

About an hour after the incident Nick and his staff gathered to talk about the altercation. During the discussion some disagreements came out – for example, why can't a little old lady get her money back, Jo-Anne said, but someone abusive can. Nick explained the situation could have got out of hand, and those Hell's Angels don't do things by halves. There could have been a vendetta against the shop and staff, and no one would have been safe. Jo-Anne had asked why Nick didn't just call the police or at least threaten them with such action, because that might have led to a back-down by the bikers. He went on further that this would have antagonised them and they would have known that the police would not get there for fifteen to twenty minutes and by that time god knows what could have happened to them all. Carnage to property and/or staff.

Nick finally put closure on the subject and said it was a lesson learnt and, in his opinion, the only way to have dealt with the situation.

"More importantly, whose turn is it to do the teas. Bill?" indicating he wanted a cup of tea and Bill it was your turn.

CHAPTER 4

Eileen was growing into a woman; she was beautiful and had shiny red hair; a typical Irish lass with an hour-glass body that attracted the opposite sex of all different ages. The problem was her father had instructed no boyfriends outside the immediate Irish fraternity and that had caused friction in her relationship with Myles. Like her father, she had a nasty, vicious streak and was not to be crossed. She always got her own way and would do whatever it took to achieve her ambition or desires. An ongoing problem and dilemma was competing for her father's attention; she longed for quality time, just the two of them. No doubt she had his protection and care but his affection was what she craved and she would get it at any cost.

As she'd grown up, she'd wanted for nothing; at first it was a puppy, then she wanted a paddock, stables and horses and she got all this. She loved the days in her mid-teens riding the horses and her dad looking on; these were her happiest days. She wished she could turn back time and live those moments again. Christmas, birthdays and barbecues were all grand lavish social functions and Eileen was always vying to be the centre of attention, and more often than not she was. However, there were always times when the lads broke away to do things like cards or darts etc. Now it was business, dealing with the other family's broods and squabbles, and Myles had very little actual time for Eileen. It was just buying gifts to pacify her, buying her affection.

In Eileen's eyes, another problem was Seamus. He was heavily involved in the business and executing orders and this led to a lot of socialising at pubs, clubs and strip joints, which was certainly (in Myles' eyes) no place for Eileen to be frequenting. Myles dedicated a lot of time to meticulous planning and making sure no trace led to him or the family. He and the boys would work all hours. Seamus and Patrick often would go on night jobs, then report to Myles info on a job, and get clearance from him to carry it out. Patrick was the leader and number two of the outfit, but would still have to update Myles if there was any deviation from the original plan. Extortion and bribery were the main part of the business, and skimming of drug dealers. This was well known in the underworld. The drug dealers would do the trading and fight out on rival low-level gangs and turfs, and Myles would take a percentage, just because he could. They wouldn't get anything in return except authorisation to continue to trade.

Eileen's mum was her best friend and confidante in all matters and feelings. Judith would shoulder these issues, emotions and sometime tears on many an occasion from Eileen about the growing shift to it being Myles and the boys on most things. Judith could understand, as she saw less of Myles and her love for him was fading due to lack of time together.

"Mum, do you worry about Conor? He's always just sitting in the corner, snacking on crisps on his computer; it's a wonder he's not twenty stone plus. I don't know how he keeps the weight off," Eileen said.

"I do, but in a funny way I'm pleased he's at home so I can keep my eye on him. He seems happy and at least he's not involved in the dodgy side of your dad's business. He's harmless enough and he has a heart of gold. You know he loves you; he might not say it, but he does," Judith said reassuringly.

Eileen took the comments onboard but she did not have much connection with Conor or Seamus; in fact, she was getting more jealous and frustrated by the day towards the boys.

Meanwhile Myles, Patrick and Seamus were getting ready to go out. It was nearly a ritual every night: do some family business, play cards, have a few chasers then go out till the early hours of the morning. Myles was a creature of habit and went to the same haunts. If any of the rival gangs ever wanted to do a hit on him it wouldn't be too hard to find where he was.

"Judith, we're just going down the pub for some drinks and darts; don't wait up!" Myles called up as he walked out the house.

This was a coded message, meaning they were more likely to frequent the local gents' club and go to the casino. They were prone to gambling heavily at the local casino, leering and wasting hundreds of pounds. None of which Judith was best pleased about, especially the gents' club; she saw that, really, as a form of cheating.

Eileen peered through the window as the black Range

Rover skidded and sped down the driveway with great haste. It disappeared from sight within seconds. She was so sad. Why couldn't her father take her and Mum to dinner just once? Eileen thought for a moment, tears welling up in her eyes and spilling down her cheeks; she could taste the saltiness of them and she swallowed hard, so upset with her situation. She stayed at the window for a few moments, then a smile came across her face as an idea took shape in her mind of how she could be thrust into her father's immediate world.

She skipped down the hall with the plan forming in her mind. She joined her mum in the kitchen and they drank rosé wine and shorts and did some cooking for the men of the family. It would normally be traditional Irish stew and some steak and ale pies, which were their favourites. Eileen would hatch a plan; she wasn't sure what yet, but it would come to her soon. Judith and Eileen would normally crash about 12.30 a.m., feeling a bit delicate but not too bad, just enough to numb the pain while the boys were out gallivanting

As for Conor, he did not like leaving the house, so he would stay in his father's study playing his computer games and watching some horror films till early in the morning. More often than not he would fall asleep in the corner, computer and TV blaring out till his father returned. So, this was a typical night for the McGinley family.

CHAPTER 5

Nick was driving into work. He felt good about himself, driving a newish Golf GTI; yes, life was good. It was a Monday morning and as he reached the outskirts of the town where he worked the build-up of traffic began. The rain began to fall and splat against his windscreen, and his wipers were doing double time, hardly making the view visible. It was about 8.20 a.m. Nick used to aim to get in approximately half an hour before the shop opened. The traffic had ground to a halt and he was a bit behind time, but it was not the end of the world.

Bill, Daphne and Jo-Anne were in today. On Mondays Nick aimed to have all staff in just to go over the previous weeks' figures, set them goals and targets for the coming week and highlight any latest marketing bulletins or things to look out for.

It was about 8.35 when Nick arrived, and all the staff were already in. Sometimes they would get a call from the area boss on Monday morning, who would try and give them a lift and get them in the right frame of mind.

The phone rang.

"Bill, get that. Put it on speakerphone so I can talk to Phil – I just need to get my coat off," Nick commanded.

Bill moved over to the phone, flicked the switch that answered the call and put on the loudspeaker all in one touch.

"Good morning, is that you, Phil?" Nick enquired knowingly.

"Yes, morning, how the devil are you?" Phil boomed back. He did this to exude confidence, power and positive mental attitude. It was his favourite phrase.

"Good, looking forward to the coming week," Nick said, lying, but knowing Phil wanted a positive mental approach and answer.

"That's the spirit. Who's in?" Phil replied.

"We're all in."

They were all out the back, but Jo-Anne, the young part-time girl, was just in the adjacent room making a cup of tea for the troops. Unfortunately, that was how things worked – part-timers getting the worst of the jobs although they all mucked in and took turns generally, apart from Nick. He was far too important and busy to make tea. The speakerphone was in the centre of the room on a table and Nick, Daphne and Bill were milling about and answering the boss's questions, kind of like an open-air conference call, informal by this point. The boss was even having a bit of a laugh. It would not be so easy-going if they weren't currently having a good patch sale-wise.

Jo-Anne came back through, put a tray down on the same table and said, "Here's your tea."

She then followed up with a classic, legendary comment, totally oblivious to the speakerphone being on. "That creepy boss, who is it – Phil? He's not coming down today, is he?

I'm sure he's a perv. He always seems to be behind me in the stockroom when I go up the ladders!"

Nick looked at Jo-Anne and gave rampant, rapid-hand signals and gestures to shush her and pointed at the speakerphone. It didn't register and she went on.

"Who does he think he is? He's like a little Hitler and the power's gone to his five-foot-nothing body. Just cos he's in charge of twenty shops and he's got a BMW, he thinks he's god's gift. I'd rather go out with Bill and that's saying something."

Bill looked over, rather pleased with himself, not realising it was not a compliment.

"Jo, is that you?" Phil's voice came through the phone with a hint of annoyance.

Jo-Anne looked at the others and put her hands to her mouth, totally dumbstruck over what to say.

"Err, err, yes," Jo-Anne said softly.

"What was that you were going on about? A little Hitler? Hope you were not referring to me, young lady," Phil said with a firm tone.

Jo once again looked around and still did not know what to say. She was lost for words, which was a first; she was about to answer when Nick came to the rescue.

"No, no, not you, Phil, as if. She was talking about one of the security guards in the centre. Oh, and by the way she is going out with Bill. I've told them, though, I don't want it to affect their work or they will have to finish it. Oh, Phil, we've got some early punters, I'm gonna let them in. Talk later."

"All right, OK then, have a good day," Phil said, bemused

and reluctantly finishing the conversation earlier than he wanted.

Nick depressed the speakerphone symbol, thus turning it off and terminating the call. They all burst into uncontrollable laughter.

"Oh, Jo, that's up there, that was just classic Jo," Nick said proudly. "You can be excused from tea-making duties for the rest of the day – in fact, the rest of the week. I can't get over the timing. Lucky for you I don't think he heard all of it, as you were not close to the phone during your character assassination," Nick continued, trying not to laugh, as they all should have respect for the area manager. It was a blatant lack of authority on Jo-Anne's part for Phil is her superior, as the Area manager.

Nick wondered what she said about him when he wasn't about. She didn't seem to hold back. He liked, well, fancied Jo-Anne, but always felt it would be unethical to ask her out. Very awkward if she said no and difficult if she said yes, so because of both those certain outcomes he did not pursue his feelings.

"Last thing, troops, positive questioning in the sales pitch and close the deals, don't take no for an answer. Remember the add-ons and get the warranties, that's where you make the money. And another thing – no money back on items; we're not a library for electrical appliances," Nick said pleased with his analogy.

The day ended well; £3,000 in sales and a few insurances sold, now the drive home. Life was good, a bit same-old, same-old but he liked it like that; structure, routine and a few treats.

CHAPTER 6

Myles, Seamus, Patrick and a few others were in the boardroom; Jack from London was patched in on speakerphone to hear the plans. Myles was to run through a job that had been planned for approximately two months and was to be executed the next day. It was a bank job.

"Let's just go over things again. I know you might think I'm pedantic but this is why we have not been caught and, on the whole, nothing leads back to us. I've arranged a meeting with the bank manager, Mr Bennet, at eleven a.m. tomorrow. As far as the bank knows, I'm opening an account and depositing a large amount of cash due to an inheritance."

Myles continued in conjunction with his flipboard.

"Seamus and I will walk through the doors at five to, and ask to meet with Mr Bennet. At precisely ten-fifty a.m. Conor will have deactivated the CCTV inside and outside the bank. Jack will be outside directing people away from the bank, telling them there has been a power cut; this is to minimise people in the bank getting hurt, if it turns messy. It shouldn't, if all goes to plan."

Myles looked at Conor briefly, as if to say, *Please confirm everything is in hand.*

"Err, yes, Dad, it will be disabled," Conor stuttered.

"I will then have a chat with the bank guy and tell him to lead us to the vault to get the money. The code changes every day but Conor has a way of grabbing that info. These are the main details I will run through again on the way to bank tomorrow," Myles concluded.

The next day Myles, Seamus, Patrick and Jack got ready. Dressed in sharp suits, top-end shoes, clean-shaven and generally well groomed, they set off to the bank, which was about a forty-minute drive at that time of day. En route, Myles went through the details and covered possible unwanted scenarios. He did not want to shoot anyone but was prepared. Conor's calculation was there could be between £200,000–300,000 normally held in the branch.

As the black Range Rover approached the bank, they decided to park two to three streets away; no camera surveillance in the street Conor had suggested. Myles spoke to Seamus and reiterated that his best English accent was required in the bank. Seamus nodded to his dad and said he fully understood. Hopefully the lessons had sunk in.

Once inside the bank, Myles led the operation. Jack was stationed outside not to let anyone in. Patrick remained in the car and had radio contact with Myles via an earpiece if anything should materialise that could disrupt the operation.

A young man approached Myles and Seamus.

"Morning, gentleman, how can I help you?" he said.

"We have a meeting to open a new account with Mr Bennet," Myles replied politely.

The man sat them down in a private booth and walked off to get the manager. A few minutes later he came and introduced himself.

"Gentlemen, I am Mr Bennet, the branch manager and I will sort out the process of opening up your account today. You are in safe hands," he said, with an element of humour in his tone.

Myles surveyed the premises very quickly; approximately ten customers and about eight staff including the cashiers he could see and he would surmise there would be some in the back office as well. Maybe fifteen in total.

After a few seconds Myles replied, "A pleasure to meet you and thank you for handling our application personally."

"That's not a problem at all, Mr Charles," Mr Bennet said.

Myles had obviously given a false name to get the meeting arranged.

"OK, Mr Charles, do you have the documents I discussed with you over the phone: photo ID, utility bills and the bank account number of where your funds are?" Mr Bennet continued.

"Actually, this meeting is changing, the agenda is different; my agenda is different," Myles said.

"What do you mean, I thought..." Mr Bennet started to reply.

Myles interrupted and continued, forcefully but controlled.

"I'm not putting money in, I'm taking all the money you have on the premises now, today, no fuss. Do you understand?"

"Mr Charles, you are a very funny man. Just get your ID out and let's fill in the forms."

Myles held a bank brochure, slid it towards the man with a handgun underneath with the muzzle protruding slightly, and pointed it directly at the bank manager's chest. He now had his attention and knew his intention was not an idle threat.

The bank manager saw the gun and his demeanour changed in an instant; his forehead and face started to glow red, and sweat formed and began to trickle down into his eyes. He replied to Myles.

"We have CCTV and panic buttons; you won't..."

Myles interjected. "I'm done talking. If you want to see your wife again or your cashier wants to see her son again, do as I say. Your wife did not reach the travel agent's today, and your cashier Sue's son did not make it into school!" he said in a raised and articulate English accent.

"We're not fucking around," Seamus said, staring at the bank manager.

Mr Bennet looked over at the cashier, fearing what might happen if he did not follow instructions.

"Lead me to the vault and fill the bag with used notes. I want twenties and fifties," Myles said menacingly.

"The safe is controlled by a pin number that changes daily," Mr Bennet said nervously.

"I have that code and you have that code, so let's do it," Myles countered.

Myles and the bank manager got up and started to walk to the back of the bank. Seamus remained seated and the general public and the cashiers appeared not to know what was going on.

Once at the vault the manager put the code in and they both entered. There was a big safe and safety deposit boxes inside and two CCTV cameras covering all directions.

The bank manager proceeded to load up the holdall; it took about five minutes.

Myles then put a tie cord on the manager's hands and hit him over the back of the head with the butt of the gun, rendering him dazed. Myles had latex gloves on to avoid leaving any fingerprints.

Myles casually walked back on to the bank's shop floor and gave Seamus the nod to exit with him.

Once out they quickly walked back to the car. Jack the driver was sitting there waiting, engine running. Myles and Seamus jumped in and they left hastily.

Meanwhile, back in the bank, the manager raised the alarm and the police arrived about twenty minutes later. The manager gave his statements even though feeling groggy but was not prepared to give a description of Myles or Seamus as Myles had threatened to kill his wife at any time.

It transpired that the CCTV to the bank, the vault inside and adjoining roads had been disabled at 10.50 a.m. and came back on 11.50 a.m. There was no footage of Myles or Seamus at all, as if the events had never taken place. The forensic team dusted for prints; none were found. The manager phoned his wife's work, and she had arrived on time and had no encounter with anybody. Everything was normal. Mr Bennet asked Sue to ring the school to check her son was there, and he was. The only evidence was that the branch computer email had been hacked at

8 a.m. that morning, but on further investigation the IP address of the computer was an internet café, so no trace there.

The bank lost £275,000 in used notes and there was not a shred of evidence. Just one extremely intimidated bank manager, who resigned three weeks later.

CHAPTER 7

Nick had arranged to meet Wayne at their favourite haunt – The Wagon; for nearly a year, religiously they went there Friday night, without fail. They had never had any success, but if anything, they were persistent and creatures of habit did not like change. The first obstacle was getting past the bouncer, despite having told him numerous times it was his propensity to always ask their age and show him ID. It was his chance to exude power; he didn't need to; he was six foot six and built like a brick ****house.

Once in, it was customary to survey the joint and strategically stand where the ratio of girls was at its peak. They perused the establishment, trying to look at and engage some females, then found their spot. *Right*, Nick thought to himself, *sorted*.

"Wayne, get the drinks before you gamble it all away on the fruity," Nick said, fairly strictly.

"What makes you say that?" Wayne replied.

"I'll tell you what makes me say that: history, bailing you out money-wise. In fact, last Friday makes me say that," Nick said.

"OK, fair comment." Wayne walked off in the direction of the bar.

Nick waited for Wayne in a good spot; he thought there was a pillar there. Should he lean against it, put his hand on it? What was the ultimate pose to project confidence? That's what girls liked, he had read or heard on some programme. Nick looked across at Wayne at the bar; as usual he was on the periphery and half-heartedly trying to get the barman's attention. It was a struggle to get served as the barman got drawn to the pretty ladies regardless of the order in which they came to the bar.

Nick got Wayne's attention and urged him to move to the centre, near the tills. Wayne read Nick's thoughts and repositioned himself.

It seemed an eternity for Wayne to return, but he did finally come back.

"What's that? I said a pint of Castlemaine. OK, never mind, least you're back and you have some of the golden liquor, although fifty-pence worth is on the floor from your attempt," Nick quipped.

Wayne and Nick stood together talking about normal stuff: football, Chelsea and Spurs, playing football as they were both on the same side.

"Look, you only ever pass when you're going to get clattered on a tackle. Many a time I've been in a goal-scoring position and you've tried to take the whole team on," Nick said to Wayne, frustrated.

"I make calculated decisions based on the scenario," Wayne said, trying to give some science to the game.

Wayne was much better than Nick but he enjoyed it and the social scene was good after matches. Whilst drinking they both would be subtly looking at the girls as this was the main aim: to get chatting and, god willing, get a date. They also spoke about snooker and work; they were due to play snooker tomorrow.

"Tomorrow, don't forget to bring some of the money you owe me," Nick said.

"OK. Look, those girls are looking over. They're a bit of all right," Wayne said.

"Yes, not bad, not bad at all. They look a bit older than us and there's five of them, so it could be awkward for maintaining conversation," Nick said thoughtfully. "On the other hand, it could give us a better chance, good ratio."

"Yes, but what happens if we have to buy a round, a bit steep…" Wayne said, concerned.

As usual they deliberated and thought about it, went through scenarios of what they could say, who should lead etc. Finally, they agreed to take the plunge and walk over. "He who dares wins", as a famous character from a sitcom once said.

Then, at the precise moment they were about to make their move, some other lads strolled up and started to chat to the girls.

Nick looked at Wayne as if to say, *That's your fault for dithering too long*. Wayne returned his gaze as if to say, *Well, you're as much to blame*.

They both hung around, hoping, wishing the girls might blow these guys out but, no, it seemed to be going well; they were laughing, smiling, gazing at each other. On that note and mission failure they both thought to try elsewhere in the bar.

About half an hour passed and it was time for another drink; it was Nick's round this time. Luckily the place they had moved to was a bit quieter and he managed to get served pretty quickly and returned to base. He gave Wayne his drink and they spoke a bit more about work and such things.

It was approaching last orders. Nick saw a few girls and thought they were nice and they went through the same motions as earlier in the evening. This time it seemed a bit more encouraging, Nick thought to himself as one of the girls was looking over in their direction. He nudged Wayne with the universal gesture to say, *We're in here*. Wayne glanced across in the general direction of where the girls were standing.

Then one of the girls waved at them. Nick couldn't believe it, and coolly nodded and waved back and, nearly in the same motion, smiled at Wayne as if to say, *Look, I've pulled*.

He was just about to walk across then he realised the girl had actually waved at someone behind him. He felt so embarrassed. A few minutes passed and whoever she waved to wasn't joining their group.

Time was running out, Nick thought; it was going to be the same outcome as every Friday – no conversations with the opposite sex, no date. He had to break the cycle.

"Wayne, I'm going over to talk to them; what's the worst that could happen?" Nick said.

"They could blank you and tell you to piss off!" Wayne said, brutally honestly.

"It was a rhetorical question, mate; that kind of answer doesn't fill me with confidence."

Nick wandered across with his most impressive and assertive walk and poise, Wayne following him. As Nick got near them, he ended up positioned to the side of the group.

"Not seen you in here before. You come here often?" Nick said (not a lot of inspiration had come out in the earlier discussions on the best way forward).

The girl half-looked over.

"Sorry, are you talking to me? I didn't hear you," the blonde girl said, touching her ear at the same time.

"I said, do you come in here that often?" Nick repeated a bit louder.

"Yes, we have started coming in recently, as the old town's getting a bit rowdy," she replied.

"Can me and my friend buy you a drink?"

The girl looked at Nick and Wayne a bit disdainfully and said, "Oh, sorry, we are just leaving; maybe next week if you're in here. Bye!" she said and beckoned the others to make a hasty, speedy exit.

"Err, OK, see you next week!" Nick said to the blonde girl as she left hastily. "See mate, I've pulled!" Nick said gleefully

"I would hardly call that cast iron; she looked like she was pacifying you," Wayne said laughingly.

"No, no, that's a technical pull, nearly a date in fact," Nick said.

They left about 11.15 p.m. and Nick felt, or was convincing himself, it had been a successful evening. To be fair it was better than most, but he was clutching at straws really.

"See you tomorrow," Nick said as they reached the point in the home journey where they split off.

"Yes, and I will beat you tomorrow, once and for all," Wayne said.

TIME'S UP

"There's more chance of Spurs winning the league than that happening." Nick laughed as he jogged off, eager not to be home too late.

CHAPTER 8

The McGinleys were having their traditional end of week meal. Judith loved the family get-together and no one could make plans on a Friday between eight and nine p.m., not even Myles for his meetings, conference calls or late-night haunts to the casino or men's clubs. It was family night.

Myles, Eileen, Judith, Seamus, Conor and Patrick – an official brother, really, and best friend all rolled into one – gathered round the table. Judith would arrange, select and execute the delivery of the three-course meals. However, they did have kitchen staff and a Michelin-rated chef who allegedly worked at the Ritz (never confirmed) put the menu together. Judith didn't have many happy times in her current existence, but this meal was her highlight of the week. She loved to see the family, boys laughing, eating, (mixed with a few drinks), plus chatting with Eileen.

The table was laid immaculately; candles, expensive wine glasses, serviettes and a silk tablecloth that went back a few generations in the family but was still in good condition.

The dining room was huge with hanging paintings, expensive antique mirrors that, if they could talk, could tell a few stories of extravagant parties, bust-ups and of course happy occasions. There were a few family portraits and various ornaments and treasures from all four corners of the world. On one wall hung an elephant's tusk and a musket rifle believed to have been used by Oliver Cromwell in the Battle of Naseby.

"What we having for drinks then, everyone?" Judith enquired.

"How about that nice Rioja we got from South Africa the other year? That must have matured well now – bit like yourself, love," Myles joked.

Judith stared, not overly-enamoured with the joke but agreed it was a good choice. They had a waitress on hand and Judith nodded for her to go and fetch the red wine discussed.

"Do a few chasers, babe, as well, vodka-based. Cheers, darling," Seamus said to the waitress.

The waitress was about sixty so was a bit taken aback by the babe reference.

Seamus and Conor giggled at the remark and the waitress's stunned look.

Eileen was sitting next to Myles to his right and had decided tonight was the night to put her plan in place. She would wait to the end of the evening; she did not want to spoil her mum's night; well, not right at the beginning. The plan was to make a name up and hopefully it would just be a lot of searching for an invisible person and she would get Dad's attention and be central to his universe, just like how it used to be. It would then fizzle out as they wouldn't find anyone with the name; at least, that was the plan.

The first course was served, which was smoked salmon with prawns. The presentation was ten out of ten, Judith thought; maybe lost a bit on the boys but it would get eaten. Drinks arrived at the same time and the waitress poured everyone a glass of wine and gave the boys their chasers.

"Love, I'll have one of those chasers as well; be rude not to and one for Patrick," Myles said nonchalantly.

Off she trotted, obedient to the boss's commands. The conversation was flowing and some old Irish folk music played in the background. Candles were burning all over the room mixed with up-to-date dimmed lights.

"Seamus, there's a few collections needed to be made and the frighteners put on a few establishments, which I'll go through with you in tomorrow morning's meeting. You know to try and implement the English accent more – your lesson going well with Beatrice?" Myles asked.

"Yes, *The rain in Spain falls mainly on the plain* and all that rubbish. It's sinking in, I speak it often but tend to drift back into our accent," Seamus said in his best British accent.

"That's good, keep it up, you know the collections are all relying on detail and your attention to this is paramount: deal in cash, minimal meet, get the gophers and young'uns to do stuff. We have enough at the local sites who are approved for jobs," Myles emphasised.

"You said no shop talk, please pick this up tomorrow," Judith said.

"Yes, sorry, I'm twenty-four seven when it comes to money. If I wasn't, you wouldn't have those Burberry bags and Tiffany necklaces!" Myles countered. "And what about the villa in Monaco – it all costs!" he continued.

Judith rolled her eyes at Myles; money and cars were his obsession. She tried to discount the family business and enjoy her main course that had just been served – a duck and pheasant-based roast with all the trimmings the family loved.

The boys downed the chasers, had another two rounds, and a couple more bottles of wine were poured out and drunk with the meal, mainly consumed by the males of the family. It had all gone well and desserts came, and then the cheeseboard, and this was shared out with everyone being adventurous and trying a varied selection.

Patrick stood up and put a knife to his glass to get everyone's attention as if there were twenty people in the room, a bit of tongue-in-cheek behind the action.

"Myles. Myles, I love you so much and would lay down my life to serve and protect you all. I feel so welcomed by everyone here and wish us success, health and wealth for many more years," Patrick announced and then fell back into his chair; the five shots, bottles of red wine, champagne and whiskeys were taking effect.

Eileen had taken in the evening but her mind was elsewhere. When was going to be the right time to deliver the bombshell, the fabrication? She decided now was the time, after Patrick's speech. How would Dad take it, how would Mum take it? And her brothers were very protective.

"Dad, I have something to tell you that I have carried for about a week but I must tell you and Mum now." She hesitated, then continued, "I went to a party out Hertfordshire way the other week with one of the Murphy girls. We drank a lot and partied but something awful happened."

Myles was half-heartedly listening and slightly intoxicated from the drinks he had downed. "Tell me, what is it?" he said. "I won't get upset if you got into a fight; it's what we do – it's in our blood!"

"No, a lot worse. I was raped by a boy in the early hours at this house. I can't remember where it was," Eileen said, now pleased she was the centre of attention, albeit with this concocted tale.

A silence fell in the room. Everyone knew not to say anything; the next words had to come from Myles. Everyone contemplated what rain of foul language was about to fall in the room's air.

"Hold on, hold on. Someone raped you? Someone raped my princess?! *They are dead, they are fucking dead!*" Myles bellowed.

Judith burst into tears and put her arms round Eileen.

"I'm serious, they are dead, not just a maim or a kicking, they are fucking dead!" Myles continued.

Seamus and Conor looked at each other.

"Dad, we will find this bloke, whatever it takes, and when we do, we will bring him to you. He might be unrecognisable once we finish with him," Seamus exclaimed.

"No, no, don't harm him; get him here then I will deal with it – she's my daughter. I will reap retribution on this cunt!" Myles screamed.

"Eileen, do you know his name, where he lives; what does he look like?" Judith said.

"Um, he was tall, about six feet, dark hair..." Eileen said, beginning to do fake sobbing, crocodile tears.

"Do you have a fucking name? Where does he live?" Myles shouted, so incensed with this news.

"Yes, I think I remember... Nick Scott was his name, from Hertfordshire, but I forget what town he said."

Myles stood up and pointed his finger at the boys and Patrick; he was steaming with anger and it looked like the veins in his neck were going to burst. He smashed his clenched fist down on the table and a few glasses fell over.

"Find this fucker, this is now our priority. Find him whatever it takes and use whatever tactics you have to employ."

The meal and evening came to an abrupt conclusion. Judith led Eileen away to one of the rooms to have a mum-daughter chat.

"Get me the whiskey bottle and leave it at the table," Myles shouted towards one of the waitresses.

He slumped down into his chair and put his head in his hands in total disbelief of the news he had received about his baby. The Jack Russell dog was jumping all over the place as well, as if even he knew the family was upset about something.

CHAPTER 9

Nick was waiting for Wayne. He'd promised to pay a slight indent of the tab he had run up. Nick did not want to miss the opportunity, rare to say the least: a bit of payback. Wayne had a heart of gold and was very reliable in a lot of things, but on the flip side, very unreliable pertaining to money matters. They were due to play a bit of snooker, have a few laughs and flirt with the barmaid in the snooker club. *Perfect end to a day*, Nick thought.

Thud!

What the hell? He'd gone from being in an upright position to face down in the dirt and grit of the road. He could feel a pain just above his eyebrow, and blood was seeping from a wound. A large percentage of the impact had been taken by his hands, luckily, but his head had taken the remainder. Dazed, he thought this was to be an unexpected and unwanted adventure.

Nick had been knocked to the ground by two burly men and a rugby tackle, it seemed.

"Quickly, you do the hands, I'll blindfold him." A deep Irish accent.

"What's going on?" Nick asked anxiously.

A few seconds passed, blatantly ignored; some things don't change in life! And these are strangers! Certainly not friends; well, he knew a few people who play a prank but this was not one of those occasions.

"Get the back of the van open!" the Irishman's colleague screamed after a minute of doing as he was told.

Nick Scott was hurled into the vehicle like a package, not a human being. These guys did not care – it was just like a disgruntled courier on his last day at work throwing a customer parcel with the full aim of some breakages.

Doors slammed shut, the engine turned over. It was a clapped-out builder-type van, Nick thought to himself. As he got his bearings, he could feel a rug and tools underneath him. He knew from his treatment he was in serious trouble, but for what? His life was quite ordinary, plain, even boring, no secrets, no enemies (or at least that's what he thought).

After about one hour of driving they went on to a very uneven road surface; he was bouncing from side to side in the van. This was aggravating his injury more; his face was jammed against the floor of the truck and he could feel a steady flow of fluid down his face; *Must be blood*, he thought. Nick figured he could be anything up to forty miles from his comfort zone/neighbourhood.

The vehicle drew to a standstill. Nick could hear voices but couldn't make out everything that was being said. Something about "Myles is in," and "He's expecting you." The rest was just lost over the distance and being blindfolded. Off again, bumpy road then smooth surface, this time for about two or three hundred yards. The vehicle stopped, and this time the back doors were flung open violently. Nick knew this time he was coming out. He was grabbed by his ankles, one man on each leg. He was dragged out with so much force that he did not have the chance to brace himself; he couldn't use his hands to ease the fall as they were bound behind his back and *bang*! He went down on his face, again. He was put on his feet and ushered along the drive or road, still not knowing where the hell he was or what was in store for him.

Finally, he had his sight back. The blindfold was taken off. They had used gaffer tape, and he felt sure he'd lost half an eyebrow in the process of the blindfold being ripped off. It took a few minutes for him to get his balance and take in the nature of his predicament and his surroundings.

His first thoughts were that he was going to be robbed, but why hadn't they done that where they had found him and then just discarded him? He had been driven all this way; it must be for someone to talk to him about something. But what? He had not done anything; it did not make sense.

Nick deliberated for a few minutes, sure he would have to draw on whereabouts and details at a later date. He took everything in now he had his vision back, but for how long? Another part of his outlook on the situation was that he might not be leaving here alive.

If their intention was to murder him, why? What was it all about? Nick had not upset or crossed anyone. He was extremely scared of his predicament and what was mapped out for him.

He was about to find out, that was for sure. He was led down one corridor then down another. It was a huge stately building, very grand, huge stone pillars, and massive double oak doors with black iron handles.

The part of the building he was now in took on a whole new persona, not fitting the outside exterior; it was modern rather than old-looking. Through the entrance hall/ foyer, he went down long corridors but these were modern studded walls with small rooms off each side. It was more like a corporate office.

In some rooms he could see activity, people busying around dressed in shirt and ties. If anyone caught his gaze, doors shut suddenly as if they did not want a stranger to know their business. This did not make sense; his captors looked like hoodlums, even Irish travellers. How did they know this place or these people? It did not tie together. It did not connect.

Down another corridor, round the corner, on and on and on – it was like a maze. It was deceptive and huge, a bit like the Tardis on the TV show *Dr Who*, Nick thought to himself, a touch of humour in this grave episode he found himself in.

Suddenly they stopped and knocked on a huge door, which did befit the outside feeling of the house; huge double doors nearly the same height as the hallway. There was a delay that seemed like an eternity. Judgement day had finally come, he thought; all his bad doings or thoughts were going to be replayed to him, including the time he went round to Julie's garden and peered up at her window in the dusk of a summer's night… One way or another Nick was about to find out what this was all about.

"Come in, come in." Once again, a strong Irish accent.

The room was grand and long; pictures covered a lot of the wall space, expensive art, swords and guns hung on the walls and a huge glistening chandelier was the pride and focus of the room. At the end, near a fireplace, sat an elderly gentleman with black sunglasses on (*A bit strange*, Nick thought to himself, but he wasn't in a position to question the gentlemen's fashion sense).

As Nick was led nearer, he could see a scar across the top of the man's forehead and a slight tan. Either well-travelled or weathered. He was a chap who had spent a lot of money on his belly and not through cosmetic surgery – probably fine living and plenty of beer. The man looked sinister and one not to be crossed. The lighting was low: a few candles burning on shelves and a few wall lights on.

Next to the gentlemen sat a red-haired woman of about forty or forty-five. She looked as if she had expensive clothes and jewellery, but this was covering the fact that she was not an attractive woman; quite plain.

Nick had not noticed but there was movement on the opposite side of the huge room. He glanced across to see two men in their early thirties, whispering with each other. They gesticulated at him with intent to inflict damage, motioned a make-believe knife in his direction.

"Is this the guy?" the old guy, Myles, shouted towards Eileen.

"Yes, that's him, that's him all right," Eileen answered with an air of delight. She was pleased; she had her dad's attention and his protection.

"What the fuck am I going to do to you? Oh, what to do?

Pain, pain is what you're going to feel, just like I feel in my heart. I want to hang you up by your balls. You have picked the wrong gal for your bit of fun!" Myles said angrily.

Myles was there with Eileen and Patrick. People you would cross the road to avoid if you saw them in the street; people who, in a bar, you would walk the long way round to steer clear of confrontation or avoid catching their look.

"I'm going to fucking cut you ear to ear, you cunt!" Seamus yelled out and motioned towards Nick.

Patrick restrained him. "All in good time," Patrick said.

"What are you going on about? I don't know this girl," Nick said nervously. He knew he had to say something. It looked like the verdict had already been given and it was biased to the rafters.

"Shut the fuck up!" Seamus yelled again, but with more fierceness and ferocity.

"Let him speak, let him speak," Myles said, calmly knowing he was in full control of the outcome and situation. In Myles' mind, this lowly piece of scum was going to end up six feet under and no one, that is no one, would hear or see him fight for his last breath.

"My name is Nick, I live in Watford and I have never seen, let alone met, this girl—" Nick started to say.

Myles interrupted this Nick character; he could not control his feelings facing this boy/man any more.

"To be honest, it's too late for you; I'd made my mind up before you were put in front of me. This girl happens to be my only daughter, Eileen. She says you raped her and beat her up and left her for dead at a party," Myles said clinically and firmly.

"You're a sick bastard and you're going to have to live, albeit shortly, with your actions," Myles continued.

"No, no, it's a lie!" Nick was fighting for his life.

"Oh, she is a liar? You're a dead fucking man!" Myles screamed. "I'm going to make you fucking sweat. In ten days, I will find you and I will do one of two things. Kill a member of your family, or kill you. If you have proof you didn't do it, then OK."

Nick thought both of those outcomes sounded bad. What was he going to do? He had ten days to clear his name or disappear. Leaving was not an option as one of his family members would certainly die. This was heavy. He could not understand the significance of ten days. Why not finish him off here and now?

"You're gonna wish you'd never gone to that party!"

Myles and Eileen left the room via a door to the back, just past a fireplace, where the fire had nearly burnt out. As Myles left, he nodded in the direction of his son and friend. That was their cue, like two Rottweilers being let off their leash.

Out of nowhere Nick received a blow to the stomach with so much force he doubled over, and a knee in the face took him back and he was out. Blood splattered on the nearside wall and a tooth or two came out as his head crashed backwards on to the stone-effect floor. Kick after kick was administered to his face. Luckily, he did not die. His face was bruised and battered, and a mild form of whiplash was just one of his wounds.

He lay there on the floor, alone and abandoned. No one

knew he was there; the McGinley family could have finished him there and then, judge, jury and executioners.

CHAPTER 10

Nick finally came round. It could have been minutes, hours, even a day since the severe beating he'd taken. He looked down at himself covered in blood, clothes torn. Where was he?

After another five minutes he tentatively pulled himself up. Was this sadistic Irish gang still around? Were they watching him already? The only thing that was clear, and still rang in his ears, was he had about ten days to either disappear permanently or somehow prove his innocence. There was a numbing pain around his midriff, and he had a headache from hell, probably from countless kicks and falling on to the marbled floor at the mansion as he was led from the house.

His eyes could not open fully, probably swollen from kicks and punches. As he squinted, he realised he was on an embankment, just off a fairly main road. He staggered up the small incline on to the road; there was a bit of traffic so he thought it might be rush hour. It was mid-October and for the last few days there had been a cutting cold compounded by high-speed winds.

Nick started to stumble along the road, not knowing if he was going in the right direction or how far from home he might be. Then came a shrieking horn of a car. Nick jerked up and backwards all in one movement – maybe they were trying to finish him off? He darted back on the pavement and stopped for a breather. He was in desperate need of a hot drink and some food; he was starving, not knowing when he'd last had a proper meal.

Looking around he did not recognise the surroundings. Was he still there, near the Irish lair? His head was fuzzy and it was hard work to think.

Nick tried to recollect where he had been taken but couldn't remember much as it had been dark, he had been bound and in the back of a van. He could be a mile or thirty miles from that nutjob who wanted to bring his life to an untimely end. He finally managed to walk but not knowing where he was heading – it just seemed the right thing to do.

Ahead he saw some signs for Rickmansworth so was not too far from home. Not surprisingly he did not get any hospitality or food from the nutty Irish gang. In the distance was a corner shop. *Great*, he thought, *I can get some bits to eat and drink.* This was one time he did not care; he was grateful for the convenience, hence the name for these types of shops.

Nick entered the shop and got a strange look. He walked around the narrow aisles; they try to pack so much in. *Pack it high, watch it fly*, as one of his old bosses had once said.

"You all right, mate?" the shop owner said concerned

Nick thought, *Why's he asking me if I'm all right? Normally, it's a "hello" or "afternoon, sir".* It confused him and he continued to look around the shop. Then the owner followed him as if he thought Nick was a potential shoplifter. This began to infuriate Nick and he turned round and snapped towards the owner.

"What's your problem? I've just come in to buy a few bits, no fuss; just back off. I'm not in the mood."

"It's just your face and your eye. You had an accident?" the owner enquired.

Then Nick realised it was just genuine concern as he looked beaten badly. Just for a moment he forgot his face was all smashed up from his unwelcome meeting with Myles and co.

"Oh, sorry, yes. I had an unfortunate run-in with my girlfriend's ex. I'll be OK. Thanks for asking," Nick said. He didn't really want to give the real story; maybe the owner was connected to the Irish mob. His mind was racing with lots of different possibilities.

He got his bits and left the shop and took a walk in the direction of where he thought a bus stop was. The road looked familiar; he was sure he had come down it one time to take his mum to a chiropractor. Nick thought about his mum – what was she going to say about his face, and his staying out overnight without letting her know where he was? He was nearly more frightened of her than this Myles figure. He laughed inwardly about his new dilemma he found himself in: which was worse – his mum or this Myles character, even though he knew really where he would rather be.

How was he going to prove that he had nothing to do with this? Should he tell his mum what happened? Should he go to the police? His mind was spinning, he didn't know what to think or do.

Before he knew it and nearly walking on autopilot, he reached the bus stop. A bus would be here for his town in fifteen minutes.

On the bus, Nick gazed out of the window, looking one way then the next. Trees, buildings, cars rushed by; he felt he was in a nightmare and hoped he would wake up any moment soon to find out that it was all just a horrible dream. His mum would be calling down that she had done him some scrambled eggs to set him up for the day. Nick's mum was such a family person – her husband and her boys were her world.

Nick thought he might move away, go up to his aunt's near Manchester, that would be the best thing. Then he realised he would be tracked down; no, the only option would be to go to the police.

The bus pulled into town, Nick flagged down a taxi and went home. He had no idea or concept of time; he'd forgotten to ask the shop owner or the bus driver.

As Nick entered the house, his mum approached him to ask him where he'd been.

"You've been out all night – that's not how I raised you! You should let me know when you're not coming home, I've been worried sick. Actually, turn round and come closer to me," his mum said.

Nick reluctantly walked towards his mum.

"What the hell has happened to you? Look at your face, it's awful. I need to look at that for you!"

"Oh, some idiots jumped me and my friend after we left the club. I'd had a few so I stayed with a friend; I'll tell you more later once I've had some sleep," Nick said wearily

When he got to his room he flopped down on the bed. A recollection came back to him – Myles saying as he was dragged out, *I know where you live, where your mum works and I know your nephew's nursery. My people have been gaining info for me. See you soon.* The voice was his last memory, hazy and foggy as he drifted into unconsciousness at the time.

He fell asleep with these nightmares going through his head.

CHAPTER 11

Nick had weighed up all his options, and knew he had to tell the police. He could investigate himself but it was too dangerous, and he had nothing to go on. He paced up and down his garden. It was Sunday afternoon about 4 p.m., the next day of the so-called ten, it was a bit cold but he just needed peace and fresh air.

He kept going over in his mind if he had been anywhere but no, definitely not, and he'd certainly not been in the company of any girls (he would remember that), plus he didn't get invited to parties – he was always on periphery of things like that.

He desperately wanted to confide in Wayne but thought better of it for the time being; maybe he'd talk to his mum. What was going to happen? Was he going to get taken out one night, would this Myles go against his word and just order the hit? He had hardly slept since the episode and what sleep he'd had was disjointed.

This girl; why had she made up such an evil story, what was her gain from it all? These questions were just stacking up like an endless conveyor belt in his mind. Rape was such a disgusting offence and would never enter Nick's mind. Like any adolescent male he had sexual thoughts sometimes when he saw a nice girl but that was only natural.

"Nicholas, what are you doing? Do you want a cup of tea?" his mum called out from the window.

"No, Mum, I'm fine, I've got things on my mind," Nick replied.

"A cup of tea rights the world in more cases than not," said his mum.

Nick didn't know where she got those sayings from; he was sure they were made up on most occasions. However, he liked them, and he liked the sanctuary of home, especially in these times.

He could not recollect a lot about the encounter: broad Irish accents, different rooms, and he was sure one was like a classroom and someone had been teaching diction and elocution. It was a blur, what was truth, what was he visualising? It was getting cross-contaminated. Fact and fiction were merging into one. He had had a lucky escape, but recollecting was foggy, and the kicking afterwards probably did not help matters. He thought the name Myles had been mentioned but was unsure.

Enough was enough; he would have to go down to the police station. He popped back inside, and saw his mum preparing dinner, peeling spuds, washing vegetables etc.

"I've got to pop out, Mum; only be an hour." He paused and looked back; she was still going about her business. She would probably make a walnut cake. He loved that, so was eager to get back later.

"OK, make sure no longer! Doing a roast, you need building up a bit," his mum said.

Nick ran upstairs, grabbed his car keys, galloped back down and out the front door. He felt relieved he was doing something about his predicament. He jumped in the car and it took its customary two tries to start. Off he drove to the town centre and the police station. It was Sunday, so he could park on yellow lines, which would save time.

Once parked, he was only fifty yards from the station. He trotted up and went in, wanting to avoid nosey people or gossip just in case someone knew him. He went up to the desk where a female officer was.

"How can I help you?" she said politely.

"I need to report my life being threatened and a kidnap," Nick said.

"OK, sir, take a seat and someone will be with you shortly."

The policewoman went out back and relayed the message to a colleague. She then came through and said someone would be out in ten minutes.

After fifteen minutes a policeman beckoned him through a side door, and he led him along the police station to a room at the back. They went in and sat down. It was a bit dingy and there was one small window. *A bit claustrophobic*, Nick thought.

The policeman completed the usual formalities of his name, his address, then started asking questions about the incident.

"OK, in your own words, explain what happened and try to give as much detail as you can remember."

"OK, officer. On the tenth of October I was waiting for a friend when suddenly I was bundled into a van. It happened so quickly. I was tied up and the journey lasted about thirty minutes."

"Do you know where you were taken to – any towns, landmarks?" the policeman asked.

"No, it was dark and I was on the floor of the van. I know it was a kind of stately home. We went down a gravel path then up some big stone steps, then into this manor house." Nick was a bit nervous as he had never been in a police station, and he knew the people he was talking about were nasty.

"Continue, in as much detail as you can recall," the policeman said.

"Once out of the van they put a mask kind of blindfold over my head but I could see through the material faintly. I was pushed along through the entrance. It seemed like a marble-finished grand foyer and I noticed a big chandelier when I looked up. I was led hurriedly down the hall, and I remember going past one room and I could hear a kind of teacher asking men to pronounce and speak in a certain way, almost like an elocution lesson."

The policeman seemed puzzled, and thought that this was a professional unit, maybe higher up the food chain than he'd first imagined, rather than some small-time gang trying to make a quick turn on a kidnap.

"Go on," he said, keen to get more of a picture of what happened.

Nick continued to go through the sequence of events to the officer, who painstakingly took it down via good old-fashioned note-taking. The officer knew there was an Irish gang and the leader was called Myles, with a daughter, and they lived in a large stately home about a half-hour or forty-five-minute radius of Watford. *This could cross over into three to four counties*, he thought.

"OK, Nick, thank you for the insight and detail of the incident. We will write this up and circulate it to our colleagues in different police forces. We are aware of an Irish gang with about four to five sub gangs working all over England from Manchester, Birmingham and London. It might be you have stumbled into this world, which is dangerous for you, as you can imagine," the policeman said.

After deliberation the officer then gave his conclusion on what Nick should do.

"You need to keep a low existence, cut down on going out, tell no one, as you'd potentially endanger them. If you have any more contact or any strange run-ins, let me know, however insignificant they could be," the officer finished and then rose. This was a cue to say the interview had ended.

Nick in turn got up and the officer escorted him out of the room, then the police station. He felt relieved that the police were now involved. Hopefully this could be sorted out and he could move on with his life.

The officer went in and spoke to a secretary and said this incident could be linked to an Irish crime syndicate that Charles Dantry was investigating; he had seen some memos about it. He would file his report and send it on to relevant people.

As Nick walked to his car the rain came down very quickly and unannounced; he didn't have a coat and he was getting soaked. He picked up a jog, and as he did, two boys on BMX bikes sped past, nearly knocking him clean over.

"You idiot, you think we don't know where you've been?" one said. He must have been thirteen or fourteen years of age.

What was he going on about? He got to his car and the rain was still pounding down relentlessly; surely there could be none left in the clouds, Nick thought. He noticed one of his tyres was completely flat. That could not be right; he hadn't gone over anything on the way here, and a slow puncture would not have rendered it undrivable so quickly.

Another thing that Nick saw made him scared: there was a note under one of his wiper blades. Instinct told him it was from the Irish firm; his moves were being watched. The ink was starting to run but he could just about make out the message.

We know where you've been. Don't go back or your nephew will be dead. Things have changed: we will take care of you soon!

Nick wondered if he should go back to the police or go home and digest all this. He decided to go home and sleep on it, then make a decision in the morning. He worried about the threat to his nephew: they knew everything.

CHAPTER 12

A few days later (day four) Nick was making his way home after a pleasant meal with his work colleagues. Due to circumstances and predicament, he would make the meal a quick affair. The store had had some good performances recently, top of the region, and his boss Phil had rewarded him with an extra hundred-pound bonus. He indicated it would be a nice gesture to spend it on a meal with his team.

Nick went ahead with the boss's notion, and invited the team out for dinner. It did cover the majority of the bill; he chose not to mention the best part had been put up by the area manager. They did not need to know that; they could just think Nick was a sound boss and was rewarding them for their hard work and endeavours.

As Nick was driving along, he was pleased he had been controlled and not flirted with the drink-drive limit; he had done that in the past, but felt guilty, plus he knew he couldn't afford to lose his licence – he would get caught one day, it's the law of averages. The meal was at a nice quaint retreat on the outskirts of Ruislip set in nice grounds and with the chef cooking all dishes to perfection. He was pleased the total bill was £180 for five of them including drinks, which Bill had taken advantage of. Bill did look discoloured in the face towards the end of the evening; anaemic, in fact. Nick could picture him having a long meeting with the toilet that night. He sniggered inwardly.

Nick knew the route by heart and started to drift into autopilot, which was not good as it only took a slight loss in concentration to end up paralysed, or even worse, dead. His mind was preoccupied with his recent run-in. The drive was tedious, taking him on long stretches of A-roads with no other cars. As he went along a slow drizzle started and visibility was tainted by the combination of that and the darkness.

After a few minutes he noticed headlamps in his rear-view mirror, but he did not think anything of it. The road was so long the vehicle would go out of sight, then come back due to distance and dips in the road. Despite the road being winding the vehicle was catching him up slowly but surely. Nick was trying to pick up pace as he didn't like cars just hanging on his lights in the dark, and using him as a guide through the difficult driving conditions and twisting roads.

Rain was now lashing down, causing him to up the wiper speed to double, which could be quite mesmerising, he thought.

The car was now right behind him, and he was frustrated with the situation he found himself in. On closer study through his rear mirror, it looked like a police car. All of sudden there was the noise of a siren. Nick slowed down and started to drive as sensibly as possible, just assuming the police car wished to pass him. The car just remained and started to slow as well.

This was strange and not right, Nick thought to himself. He had committed no offence; his car was all in order and if they wanted to check his documents, they would find them all in order and up to date.

The car blinked its headlamps a few times; the blue lights were flashing and sirens were still blaring so Nick took this as a sign the police wanted him to slow down and pull over. After what had gone on last week, this seemed too coincidental; he thought this was linked to his kidnap last weekend.

A policeman got out of the car, which was parked about ten or fifteen yards behind Nick. He heard a *rat-a-tat-tat* on his driver's window so he wound it down and looked up at the officer.

"Would you like to get out of the car, sir?" he said and stepped back slowly. It was OK, it was genuine, Nick thought.

"Is it not something we can discuss whilst I'm sitting in the car?" Nick said politely, not in a confrontational manner.

"No, it's not – get of the car now!" shouted the policeman, his voice raised in the tone of a sterner deliverance.

Nick got out of his car. He now noticed a second police officer (well, he presumed he was a police officer) get out of the car and start to walk towards them in a slow, deliberate manner. Why had the policeman taken that tone? It looked like he was being targeted, but for what reason?

"I'm Officer Burton, and this is my colleague, Officer Robbins," the policeman said.

"Evening, sir," came from the other policeman in a fast manner, with a slight hint of an Irish accent.

Nick twigged what was happening; was this it? His execution? Had they change their minds – no leniency? His mind was racing at a hundred miles an hour; there were so many things he had never done. He had only had sex with two different girls; never seen Chelsea win the league; never taken his mum on their dream holiday – a trip on the Orient Express. Never…

"You were speeding," the officer said unreservedly.

"No, I wasn't," Nick protested.

"You were!" exclaimed the officer with the Irish accent.

A couple of vehicles were coming down the road. They seemed to come from nowhere, even off the verge, and slowly approached.

The first policeman gesticulated to the vehicle to slow down.

He spoke with the driver. Nick could not make out any faces – it was extremely dark and the rain obscured any distinctive features of the driver.

They continued to talk for a few minutes and the (so-called) policeman looked back every now and again towards Nick. The conversation finished and the vehicle sped away quickly. Nick noticed it had no plates, and wondered why it had gone off at such speed, especially in front of the police.

The policeman walked back over to his colleague who was still with Nick. He pulled him over and had a little chat out of Nick's earshot. He still could not believe the sequence of recent events in the last four days and he was not sure what the outcome was to be now or over next few days.

"OK, you can go," Officer Burton said, then casually started to head back to his car.

"Excuse me, what force are you from?" Nick asked.

"Why?" the officer said abruptly and annoyed.

"Just curious," Nick said, knowing his rights or at least he thought he did.

"We work out of Middlesex police division and are based in Uxbridge, sir."

Nick glanced up and took a mental note of the police number on the officer's lapel and shoulder. It was 6772.

Both policemen jogged back to their car due to the downpour of rain. Nick got back in his car and decided to wait for them to go off first; he did not want the hassle of policeman vetting his driving performance. He had a pen and paper and quickly jotted down the policeman's name, rank number and number plate before it went out of sight.

The police car was gone so he turned the engine over and started to head home. As he drove back, he could not help wondering if this was a message from his new Irish acquaintances; that they could reach him wherever and whenever.

Maybe he had seen too many films, and his imagination was running riot, but it just did not add up, this random pullover, it was too coincidental. This Officer Robbins had an Irish accent, and he had never come across an Irishman with the name Robbins. It was probably all correct, but he would visit the police station tomorrow nonetheless, just to clear his paranoia.

Nick finally got home about 1.30 a.m. and went straight to bed. He could not sleep; his mind was working overtime. There was a bunch of Irish nutters and they intended to kill him in five or six days. Time was running out, and this evening's events proved that they could get to him whenever they wanted to. Deep down he knew that was what they were going to do. Nick thought they would not want to compromise their reputation, plus they wanted to avenge the girl's so-called rape. Why was she lying?

He would have to go to the police, especially if this evening's incident proved to be linked to his kidnap last week.

CHAPTER 13

Myles and Seamus had some catching-up to do. They decided to go to their normal haunt – a gentlemen's club on the outskirts of London. They were driven up by one of their drivers. Once dropped off, they told the driver to come back about midnight.

In the club they were given a roped-off section, kind of a VIP area as if they were celebrities; they were gangsters to be feared, and thus given special privileges. After a few minutes a couple of bottles of champagne were delivered to their table and a few blondes in minimal clothing arrived shortly after. Myles would expect this service and was accustomed to it, whether it was at a restaurant with his wife, drinks and tea at the Ritz or a seedy gentlemen's club.

Myles was talking business with Seamus, and advised about a big score that was going on that Terry (one of Myles' key men in London) was planning. It was to be a large heroin haul and the exchange was happening in Terry's manor in London.

"This job is big, and Terry and Jack have had some inside knowledge of the numbers involved. We're talking six figures and minimal work. Just go in, knock them all out, and take the winnings," Myles smiled to Seamus.

Seamus thought killing people might not be hard for his dad but certainly horrible for him and hated this aspect of the job. However, it was the business he and his father were in.

Myles swiftly changed the subject away from that side of the proceedings back to family problems, notably Eileen's vengeance.

"Seamus, I can't let this Nick guy distract our purpose and operations. No more time, just find him; I want you to finish him off. Kill him, and I want it to be a family member to do the retribution. I want you to fire the fatal bullets. Take a few boys, go to his town and sort it in the next few days."

"Dad, no problem, but you know we only have Eileen's word on this?" Seamus said hesitantly. Although he put on the gangster image/show he only liked the rewards, not the dirty work and killings. He had, nevertheless, carried out a few hits already at his tender age.

"Look that's enough for me," Myles said.

They sat and drank and had some laughs with the girls. The place was getting busy and there was a lot of noise. Usually, they would stay for a few hours, and some talk was done about work but this rape allegation was burning on Myles' mind. He had to right the wrong and would only accept blood as recompense.

"I'm going for a few dances; keep a low profile, drink and have some fun with a few of the girls," Myles continued, and he headed off into the shadows of the club to a booth, drink in one hand and a brunette in the other. Myles loved his life and he didn't see this as cheating on Judith, just a bit of fun. The old adage *boys will be boys*.

Seamus was having a few drinks and flirting, touching up the girls. He was a little overweight and sweated easily and quickly. One of the girls he was with didn't like the way he was touching her and motioned one of her regulars to come over and rescue her.

It was an Asian lad and he came over and asked if she wanted to go to the bar and get a drink. The girl started to stand up and Seamus pulled her down firmly.

"Oi, she wants to come with me; she's spent time with you – let her go," the young man said.

An undercover policeman working in the Detective Scrivener squad was tracking the McGinleys and was in the establishment. He moved closer to the fracas. He had an audio recorder on him and recording dialogue. *You never know*, he thought, *they might finally say something incriminating.*

Seamus rose from his seat. He was about six foot two and sweat was starting to run down his face. He looked at the boy and if looks could kill… Security in the club was drawn to the scene. They were there mainly to stop men touching the girls inappropriately, and a skirmish between blokes was rare.

At the very same time Myles was returning to the table and the girl he'd had a dance with had gone off to the ladies room.

Seamus shouted, "Do you know who you're dealing with? I take people like you out for fun, buried, never to be found again. Dumped in rivers without trace. Why don't you fuck off?"

"You don't scare me," the lad said. He was quite athletically built. Whilst this was kicking off, the undercover cop was recording it all and had a concealed camera rolling in parallel with his audio device.

Myles heard the fracas and could see Seamus in the centre of it all; he quickly realised they didn't need this attention. It was too late.

SMACK.

Seamus laid the lad out with one punch. He went crashing backwards on to the table, which smashed and glasses were sent in all directions. The girls in the club scurried away to their room or out the back.

"You don't mess with the McGinleys!" Seamus screamed proudly.

Myles grabbed Seamus and pulled him away. They barged past onlookers and security and straight out of the club.

"Seamus, what were you thinking? Anyone could have been there; the boy might go to the police!" Myles said furiously. "You know the police are aware of us but have no evidence and we pay a lot of detail to keep it that way, money put in place to leave no trail. If you weren't family, I'd have you off the firm," Myles concluded.

Myles gestured to their waiting driver across the road. The car came quickly, they jumped in and sped off.

Meanwhile, in the club, the policeman had some good evidence, and finally he could report back to his superiors. This was the breakthrough they needed. The Asian boy got up, bloody-nosed and with one less tooth. He went over to security and spoke with them. The outcome was they advised him who he'd had a run-in with and persuaded him not to take it further.

CHAPTER 14

"Let's just look at this, shall we. You, you and you are all meant to be elite – that's a joke. Policemen, top of your profession, detectives. Yet they're doing contract killings, intercepting major drug deals between dealers and gangs, kidnappings for ransom, protection, racketeering, money laundering. Yet, no one within these four fucking walls has a lead, a link. We all know who's behind it, yet you still can't trace his living abode; how many more officers or forces do I need on this?" Detective Charles Dantry bellowed. "You need to start doing some fucking detecting."

The detectives and crime investigation officers in the room looked on, dumbfounded and speechless. Myles and Patrick's gang had been trained and briefed well, they didn't leave clues. They used contract killers, they disabled CCTV on jobs, changed cars then changed plates. On a few occasions, cards had been found but no fingerprints, no DNA, nothing. Myles' outfit was professional, with a lot of ex-military members.

Dantry's colleague, Scrivener, then interjected and continued the briefing.

"He's a cancer and he's infecting our neighbourhood and the country up and down as well. I want more groundwork. Go dirty if you have to. Only just last week we had a kidnapping, and I believe it was Myles and his cronies behind it. The family paid up in fear of violent repercussions," said Scrivener. "Let's think outside the box, see what we can unravel here. Use your brains – you're paid a handsome wage," Scrivener continued.

Dantry smashed his clenched fist down on the table. Anyone who had started to drift off or daydream was suddenly pulled back and aligned.

"It's gotta stop, and soon. There are even rumours that he has police working for him in some forces," Dantry said, looking round the room with suspicion.

"Sir, we do have one lead. Well, it could be linked," said one young officer. He had been in the Serious Crime squad for three months and was keen to get noticed.

"Well, go on, spit it out. What is it?" said Chief Detective Scrivener.

"It could be nothing," the young Officer Cook went on.

"Let me be the judge of that," Scrivener snapped back, with a hint of desperation.

"Well, the Herts force had an incident involving a few Irish men. We knew some of the gangs went to this gentlemen's club so we had one of our young detective constables do an undercover stake-out. Myles was in there with his son, Seamus. As you know we are still having trouble with their residence despite continued surveillance. The club did not report the incident and the victim did not press charges," Cook said.

"OK, go on, and please advise the room why we are having trouble with surveillance. We have Patrick's and Seamus' mugshots. What about the other son, Conor; do we track him?"

"Firstly, we have still not established the HQ. We have narrowed it down to a ten-mile radius from mobile phone interception and early-stage triangulation software," Cook said. "They have a sophisticated structure in place, plus mobiles are changed, and SIM cards are changed. Then they pass on the SIM cards to the general public in other towns that then throws us off track." Cook went on. "They also use army satellite phones for communication and they can't be traced – they pay a lot of attention to detail to not be listened in to, followed or caught on their jobs.

"The son, Conor, is believed to be deaf and dumb or have some type of mental condition and he isn't involved in any of the family criminal activity. He has been photographed at a family function when they went up to London; that is all."

"Anything else, any other leads?" Scrivener asked.

"Another incident where a young male was kidnapped and threatened. He said the name was Myles, so it's probably the same family."

"Continue to monitor the gents' club – they're bound to gravitate back to their haunts; they will make a mistake soon, especially this Seamus. He's a big head," Dantry said with a sense of hope, trying to remain positive.

"As for the kidnapping, pull that report from the relevant police force and add it into our library info of the McGinleys. This potentially is the first mistake they have made that will lead us to them and find out where their operation is, and from there we can establish the extent of their reach and network. I believe they are working in most big UK towns or have affiliated gangs," Dantry finished.

Dantry was under intense pressure to get some leads. Nothing had materialised in regards to leads so far and officers higher up and senior management were questioning his credibility to handle the job. Quite a lot of money had been allocated to the investigation and they still didn't have any concrete evidence to incriminate, didn't know the HQ. However, Scrivener and Dantry knew they were the instigators and perpetrators of hits, kidnaps, intimidation, racketeering, drug deals and murder.

Scrivener had to turn something up, and maybe the altercation the Irish lads had had at the gents' club could be vital and the first steps in their pursuit. He had a gut feeling that twenty-four-hour surveillance would turn something up. But it needed to be jumped on and he knew he had to throw a lot of resources at it.

Dantry ended the briefing. "Get some people to talk to this Nick again, keep watching him as they will want to get him soon if their threats are to believed."

CHAPTER 15

"You need to find the fucking meet ASAP, there's two-hundred thousand up for grabs, and thrown in for the good, four less fucking Scousers!" Jack screamed at his right-hand man, Terry, in the boardroom at Myles' house. Jack was head of a lot of UK operations, was based in London and was the major interface to Myles and Patrick on all jobs and hits etc.

No hit went down or got signed off unless Jack had given a strict 100 per cent seal of approval. The last six to nine months they'd been reducing hits. They just wanted to stick to intimidation, bribery and scaring the fuck out of people. Intercepting drug deals was a major part of the business at the moment. They intimidated and robbed the drug dealers in the UK; let them take the risk then take them down after the event.

Jack was one of only two Englishmen on the firm and worked closely with Terry. There was a reason for this – Myles and Patrick liked business kept in the family. Myles found it hard to let the Irish/British conflict go to one side, even in business. Jack, however, knew the streets, he had contacts and was not afraid of anything or anyone. In a fight he never knew when to throw in the towel. He was like a Jack Russell and a piranha fish all rolled into one.

"It's going on down near their manor. The cockneys are going up, with the full intention of taking the dosh and the drugs," Terry replied, fully informed.

"Like winner takes all, the Scousers probably suspect something; there has been bad blood on other deals in the past." Jack replied

" I think it's going to be near Toxteth;" Terry continued, "they've got a serious arsenal of firepower and we will have to be well tooled-up."

"No, we don't; Cyril the sniper will have them all down in the blink of an eye. Take some muscle as backup nearby, but you won't need it, trust me," Jack said convincingly. Jack had seen Cyril's work on a few occasions – he left nothing to chance and no trace. Cyril was an ex-paratrooper and had all the nous and experience for a job like this. He revelled in the meticulous planning and thrived on the perfect execution.

Terry hadn't heard from Jack for a few days; this was not uncommon with these deals – they took a bit of finalising, lots of reconnaissance and plans had to be laid.

Another commonality to factor in was both gangs were drug addicts and could be out of their heads for days on end. In the addict's world, one day merges into another. They got up in the afternoon then went out looking for their prey in the evenings. They knew the usual suspects, their haunts and where they frequented.

The Scouse gang was headed up by a Scot (how crazy was that, Terry thought). Alex was his name and he was very flash with his money; it was a small miracle he had not already been a target for a drive-by (in this industry), when one gang steals another's gear and cash all in one hit on a meet. Alex was in his early forties and an ex-football hooligan; that was where he made his name and reputation, and he was well feared through the majority of Liverpool.

As for the London crowd, they were opportunistic and were very untrustworthy with a bit of history for being untoward to drug dealers. They were in Liverpool in a safe house; one of their lot had some digs and was the general spy and lookout for day-to-day business. Bow was his nickname as he was brought up and raised near St Mary-le-Bow church. This, in the cockney fraternity, made him the ultimate *Del Boy*.

Bow was prone to missing days here and there due to excess usage of drugs. He had finally arranged to meet up with Alex in a local nightclub. Bow and Alex had done some small deals before locally and Alex tended to take liberties as he had backup and was on his own turf. However, this time it would be a bit different.

They entered the nightclub. The music was late eighties: New Romantic, like Culture Club, Wham and Duran Duran. It was loud, and there was a haze of smoke gathering in clusters all over the club. Alex was sitting down at a table with a few of his men and a couple of local girls. The type that hangs around for free drinks, gets verbally abused then gets upset and moves on to the next group of boys.

It was about 11.30 p.m. and Bow turned up to arrange the rendezvous for the deal between the two gangs. He strolled past the queue and nonchalantly walked past the security guard.

"Oi, hold up, mate, there's a queue!" someone mustered the courage to say as they were patiently waiting in the pouring rain.

"Yes, I know, you cunt, and…?" Bow casually said, walking back towards the guy. Bow glared at him.

"You've piped up, giving it the large one; you gonna do something about it?" Bow continued, really intimidating the guy. The guy looked away and could not hold eye-to-eye contact; he knew he was in an uncomfortable position. He was luckily saved.

"Bow, come through; leave it, it's not worth it," the bouncer said, trying to defuse the potential flare-up. He knew that Bow would not let up or give up. He pulled Bow back and guided him towards the front of the queue.

Bow paused, turned round and looked at the guy one last time.

"You've had a touch," he said and strolled on without so much as a second glance. The rest of the queue eased out of Bow's way; there were a few whispers but nothing that could be heard. People were not stupid.

Once in, Bow thought he would get a pint just to mellow himself out. He had been projecting confidence for years now and did not know when, and when not, to switch it off. He started to walk across the club, knowing roughly where Alex would be; he was a regular, hence the fast-track into the establishment. As he walked, he knocked a man's drink nearly out of his hand.

"Mate, look where you're going!" the man said with a slight tone to his voice.

"Shut it and look where you're fucking standing, you div," Bow shouted out, not slowing up at all and not giving the man the time of day.

Jack, the lookout for the Irish (London division) gang, had spotted Bow coming in. He had been there a few hours, and had intercepted the calls with some old army equipment from the terrorist days. He had planted a bug that had an ultrasonic high-frequency pick-up mic concealed in the base of the candle on Alex's table. Jack followed Bow.

Bow paused, looked around, then pulled up a chair. Alex's men moved aside a bit to allow the two of them to confer and sort out the meet details. It was for a big amount, hence the Irish interest. As the conversation developed, numbers were bandied about, street values, quality and quantity. Typical drug-deal language. It did occur to Jack from afar that there was no love lost between these guys, and after about ten minutes of discussions it was finished. Both knew a time and a place, and both gangs knew to have backup. It was an official rule and expectation.

Bow got up and knocked a few drinks over on the table. It flared up – one of Alex's men was on his feet and grabbed Bow. Bow pushed him back. Alex's men knew Bow's London backup was nearby, even in the club.

Alex looked at Bow. This was unlike him: he thought he would keep it civil in a public place. Bow looked at all his men as if to say, *Do you fancy your chances?*

As Bow moved away, Alex called out. "Don't mug us off like you did to the Mancs; we won't tolerate it, not on our patch."

Recently the London gang had brought up a load of cocaine but had filtered it down by fifty per cent and word had got out. Gangs in Newcastle, Nottingham – the con had rippled out. The problem was the London crowd controlled the majority of cocaine coming in from Colombia and Jamaica; they could not be cut out of the loop, as they were integral to the drug-import network.

Bow stopped in his tracks and turned round slowly. He grinned from ear to ear but still oozed assertiveness to his enemies. He walked back to the table and leant into Alex's ear.

"We'll be smart and prepared," he whispered with conviction. With that he was off. Alex tried to get his attention but Bow was gone, on a mission to communicate the info – and he needed a spliff.

Jack looked on. This was not what he expected, this much hostility, but it did not really matter; they were all dead men walking on paths and journeys to one destination, and that was six feet under.

Jack had come in with his suit on and looked like the staff in the club. "Let me replace that candle, it's nearly burnt out. Don't want to spoil the mood," he said sarcastically to the gathering at Alex's table.

"Ha ha, you're a comedian; just do your fucking job," Alex retorted with haste.

Jack took the unsuspected recording device that was concealed in the candle. Soon Jack was out the club and, on his way, back to his flat. It was all on, he just needed to get the information from the recording and feed it back, then the operation would start to take shape.

After extracting the info, he knew where the meeting between the two gangs was and the times, etc. It was going to be in a warehouse in Lewisham. He would have Cyril set up a few hours before. His MO was to take down the Scouse and London gangs then Jack and his men would collect the cash and the gear.

Jack communicated this to Myles and he gave the say-so to execute the plan Jack had set up.

Two days later both gangs turned up at 10 p.m. at the depot in Lewisham. Coincidentally both gangs had cars with blacked-out tinted windows, four members in each car. It had transpired from hearsay that the London gang had the intention of taking the drugs and not handing the money over.

Cyril was set up in an abandoned flat nearby, two rifles loaded for quick fire. Jack was on the ground with his colleague, both with hand pistols to tidy up if anyone was not taken out by the sniper.

Both gangs got out of their cars; there was about thirty yards between the vehicles and both pointed to each other and gesticulated, then it calmed down. After some small talk and finalisation one member from each gang walked to the middle. One member of one gang with the money, one with the drugs just to do the exchange. It was very tense, both sides not trusting each other.

Jack saw all the members on both sides; he had surveillance

and pictures of the members of both gangs on his computer and in his mind. He looked up at Cyril to give the thumbs up. This meant take the shots as soon as you can.

A minute elapsed. Raised voices were being exchanged between the rival gangs; Jack looked up again – why hadn't Cyril reeled off the shots?

Then a rain of shots was fired in quick succession. Five of the seven went down, instantly dead. Jack stepped out of the shadows and finished the remaining two off. It was clinical from Cyril and Jack. Jack noticed one left in the car, went over and shot him in the forehead – gangland execution.

He beckoned over his colleague. They both had balaclavas on just in case CCTV was on around the venue. They collected the money and drugs and ran off. Cyril loaded up his guns into a bag and he disappeared into the night like a fleeting ghost.

Jack thought it had gone to plan perfectly. Myles would be pleased.

CHAPTER 16

Nick could not handle this; his brain and mind were buzzing, he had to tell a friend of his plight. It was coming up for a week now since the kidnap. What the hell was he to do? He felt like his life was slowly sifting out like the sand in an hourglass, sifting continually, grain by grain. These mad Irishmen, with no evidence apart from a jumped-up Irish girl's allegation, were going to cancel his life within ten days, well, four now as six days had passed.

It was no good, he had to talk to someone about this. Not necessarily to get any advice but just to share his feelings, get it off his chest. He had a few friends, but probably the best for this bombshell would be Wayne.

Wayne was a good lad with a heart of gold, just misunderstood mainly by the opposite sex, apart from his mum who worshipped the ground he walked on. Nick called him and asked if he fancied a game of snooker. It was about six in the evening, so hopefully Wayne would be up for it.

"Er, Nick, I'm a bit knackered and I'm short of some readies," Wayne said pathetically. It was an ongoing problem; he never had any money, always gambling. Nick was frustrated but he had to get him out at any cost, literally. He could sense it would not take much, just the lure of saying he would lend him some money. It had to be done.

"I will lend you some dosh. I need to get out, I have got some bad news to talk about, serious shit," Nick proclaimed. Wayne could sense the urgency in Nick's voice and knew not to say no – *And a few drinks would not go amiss*, he thought.

"Yeah all right, what happened to you last Friday? Anyway, I'll see you at the bar about eightish. I might even beat you this time!"

"I will tell you what happened, really heavy shit, I'm down at my lowest point in a long time, but even in this state I will beat you. Even at my worst it's still better than your best." Nick sniggered down the phone. He was not sure how he still had a sense of humour. His life felt like a game of hangman and he was on the verge of hanging in a couple of moves.

"Don't let me down; be there!" he said, finishing the conversation and hanging up the phone. Wayne thought he best go.

Nick got there a few minutes before Wayne, so he arranged to pick out the table and balls. It was a typical snooker hall, dark and the subtle hint of smoke fumes lingering above some of the tables. The club had about twenty tables in four rows of five, or five rows of four depending on which way you were looking at it.

"Tracey, what's the best table left, without any drift?" Nick enquired.

"You think you are professional now?" Tracey laughed.

"I do try – I got a fifty-four break a few weeks ago," Nick said proudly.

"You should join the club's team or enter one of the competitions," Tracey said encouragingly.

"I've got a lot on my mind at the moment, plus I don't want to upset the old boys on the team," Nick said, closing that subject down.

"Anyway, back to the original question, probably thirteen is the best of what's left," Tracey said with a touch of flirting. Whether that was for Nick or she did that for all the customers, either way he felt quite good about it and smiled back.

"Yep, OK, thirteen it is. Unlucky for some; if I lose it will be your fault," he quipped, gazing into her eyes momentarily. Tracey was a bit of a looker, but dressed a tad tartish for Nick's liking. Still, she was easy on the eye, as they say.

Wayne came in and went over to Nick. Wayne looked a bit perturbed and had a stern look of concentration for once. Normally everything was a laugh and a joke to him.

"Hi, mate, you sounded stressed on the phone. What is it?" Wayne asked, not knowing what he was about to hear back.

"I'll tell you later," Nick said, cutting it short and choosing the right moment and surroundings to discuss his recent episode with the Irish mob.

"Hi, Trace, a pint of Beck's and a pint of Foster's for the wimp." Wayne always said this as Nick had the Australian weak lager instead of the stronger German beers Wayne normally had.

Tracey poured the drinks and handed them to Wayne. Nick settled up, including the deposit for the table. He always wondered about that; they were paid-up members not novices, and yet they paid a deposit for some shitty tables that had seen better days,

They strolled over to the back of the hall, passing several tables with games going on. It was not competition night, so most games looked relaxed with a hint of casualness to them.

Nick and Wayne got to their table. They put their glasses down and set about putting the balls in the relevant places. Nick basically racked up the reds in the triangle and Wayne put the colours on the correct spots.

The table was set and Nick was chalking his cue. Looking around, he gestured for Wayne to come closer as he was going to start the serious conversation off.

"Wayne, I'm in serious trouble. You promise not to tell anyone? If you do, you could quite simply put your life at risk," Nick said seriously.

Wayne started to form a smirk across his face and spoke. "What are you on about? What is it?" Wayne replied half-heartedly.

"No, listen, mate," Nick said abruptly and hopefully bringing Wayne back to the severity of his position. "My life was threatened just last week by some fucking half-witted Irish gang."

"You've been watching too many gangster movies. What you on, I'll have some." Wayne steered the conversation away and went on, "Tracey was looking pretty hot tonight; I would, given the chance."

"Shut up and listen. I will tell you what happened," Nick said, steering it back again. Wayne cued off, not very well, getting the white the wrong side of the blue. Nick smirked as Wayne left a fairly easy red as an opener.

In between shots Nick told Wayne what had happened, about the people he had met and the mansion he had been taken to during his kidnap. As Nick retold events it hit home what a bad situation he was in.

After Wayne's initial reaction that it was a wind-up, he understood this was no joking matter. He realised his best friend was in trouble and there was nothing he could do to say or help. He felt helpless and frustrated but tried to reassure Nick that talking to the police about the matter was the best thing to do.

Nick reiterated he had not committed the rape and did not know the girl. He explained he had given a statement to the police and noticed some protection at his house, some police car out the last few nights.

"I know you probably didn't do it," Wayne said jokingly.

This got Nick's back up.

"*I didn't do it!* No probably about it!" Nick shouted as loudly as you could in a snooker club.

"Sorry, that's what I meant," Wayne corrected himself.

Nick and Wayne played a few frames and Nick, for once, was losing. Very unusual; he never lost to Wayne but with his current dilemma constantly nagging away at him it was hardly surprising. Added to the fact that whatever he did went wrong, and Wayne was definitely getting the run of the balls, which always helped. Nick felt whenever he came to the table the ball was either close or under the cushion, which always made a shot more difficult.

It was a bad night. Nick lined up a pot, then felt a cue go into his side. He was not in the best of moods and was just about to mouth off at the offender, but thought better of it. It was a snooker club and despite not having the etiquette of a golf club it still had a bit of decorum and some rules.

"Sorry, mate, it was a genuine accident. Did it muck up your shot?" It was a half-hearted and lame excuse for an apology from an Irish bloke. There was an edge of arrogance in his tone.

Nick's first thought was not about the lack of sincerity in the apology, but the bold, broad Irish accent. He could not believe it – they were in Hemel, in his snooker club. Come to think of it, he did not recognise these lads. Paranoia. Once it sets in, you can't get it out of your mind.

Nick started to try to be rational; there were a few Irish lads who frequented the club and there was a travelling community at the back of Hemel in Cherry Tree Orchard. That was it; he was just being stupid and he thought no more of it – well, tried not to.

Wayne was feeling a bit parched and after finishing his shot said, "I will get the drinks in: JD and Coke or a pint, mate?" He was a little bit on a high. "I'm finally going to whip your butt on the green bays. Look at the score line – read it and weep!"

"Yes, JD and coke; can't do a pint again, here's twenty for the rest of the night-pay me back another time," Nick returned.

It was bad, Nick thought to himself. He was about twenty points down in this frame, which was a lot at their level of snooker and one frame adrift as well.

Nick looked at Wayne and his look indicated *Yes, go and get a round in.*

"Oh, and don't ask Tracey for crisps," Nick said with a hint of a snigger.

It was a running gag – as the crisps were high up, and she had to use the little step-stool, if she had her short skirt on (which she normally did) and you got the right angle, you would be guaranteed an eyeful.

As Wayne went over to the bar Nick was left alone, and suddenly the only people he could see or hear in the hall were the Irish lads. Their laughing was becoming like an everlasting ringing, getting louder and louder by the second. Every now and again the Irish lad who had knocked him looked round and just gave a wry grin as if to say, *Well, what you going to do?*

"Pint of Beck's and a JD and Coke, please," Wayne asked politely, trying to engage more conversation with her.

"Your mate, he usually has Foster's; why's he on the shorts?" Tracey said inquisitively.

"Not sure," Wayne said, uninterested especially as she was talking about Nick's change of drinking habits.

"There you go, luv; anything else?" Tracey enquired.

"Oh, and a packet of…" Wayne paused. "No, actually, don't worry about it," he said, having been very tempted to ask for a packet of crisps, even though he wouldn't have eaten them.

Nick was hoping Wayne would be back – it seemed he had been gone for ages but it was only a few minutes.

As Wayne approached the table, Nick greeted him with his nagging observation.

"Those guys over there, they're Irish," said Nick, hoping it would click with Wayne, but the link was lost on him.

"Yeah... and?" Wayne replied and sipped his drink, somehow at the same time.

"Have you not been listening for the last half hour? They're here, trying to put the frighteners on me, sending a message of intent."

They continued playing and Nick forgot about the Irish lads, played a few frames and finally got back in the lead. Normality was restored. He had been in danger of losing for the first time in a while to Wayne. Having said that, Wayne could play in fits and starts; he was on a bit of a break for their standard. In fact, Wayne had knocked in a few balls in a row and Nick was surprised but pleased in a way.

Wayne came away from the table after his little break, smirked as if to say *What do you think of that?*

"Not bad," Nick said.

"On the scoreboard, am I top or bottom?" Wayne said, proud of his little knock.

"Yes, you are still bottom; very apt," Nick said with a touch of annoyance. He shouldn't begrudge him his bit of glory from his good break.

"What was that, thirty-one? Yeah, three blacks and a pink," Wayne said knowingly and proudly. It was normally Nick who could put that kind of break together.

Nick looked around and noticed the Irish lads had gone. Maybe it had just been a coincidence and there was no link to the other night. He felt at ease for the first time in the evening.

They played one more frame and Nick took it quite convincingly with breaks of thirty-two and twenty-four.

That was it, three-one to Nick. He felt good, even if was just beating Wayne. They put the balls away, took them back to the bar and said goodbye to Tracey. Nick felt he got a nice little smile. Maybe one day he would summon up the courage to ask her out, but now was not the time, not with his current problems.

As they walked from the snooker club, they soon parted company and went to their respective cars.

"I'll call you to check on you, all right? If you need me, call anytime, day or night," Wayne said.

"Cheers, nice one. Wayne, I'm not kidding, this is big-time bad news. This ranks as my most terrifying time. Above the Chelsea/Leeds trouble and above the Apsley boys run-in."

"What was that?" Wayne said, interested.

"I've told you loads of times; I will tell you again another time," Nick said and turned to walk towards where his car was parked a hundred yards away down a side street.

"OK, you going to shoot arrows with your dad at the weekend?" Wayne said.

Nick looked over at Wayne with a quizzical gaze. "Yes, and it's better known as archery, you fool," he said, laughing.

The walk back to his car took him past a cemetery, which was always a bit eerie. Whatever time of the year there always seemed to be thin, white smoke hovering over the graves and tombstones, Nick thought to himself, like ghosts coming out of the graves disguised as mist.

He'd already had the spooks and frighteners from the evening's encounter with the few Irish lads at the snooker club. His mind was racing. *That nudge from the Irish boy's cue was no accident*, he thought. As Nick walked by the cemetery quickly, he could hear voices, then a sudden meow.

A cat sprang up on a nearby bench and Nick nearly jumped out of his skin. *Fuck this*, Nick thought; black cats, voices from the grave and nutty Irish gang members at the snooker club, what else was going to happen?

"Oh, mate, you got any loose change for some cider?" a tramp enquired.

For the second time in literally a minute, Nick's heart skipped a beat. The man appeared from the other side (not the afterlife) of the cemetery and Nick could see him from his chest upwards. He was dressed in a tatty coat that had rips and bits of white cotton showing. Nick was not in a compassionate mood; bad timing for the tramp.

"No, I fucking haven't!" Nick shouted. "Go back to the box you have sprung out of."

Obviously, it was the tramp's new residence, not likely to get anyone stealing this pitch because of its location. Nick finally got past the cemetery and his heart rate slowed back down again to an acceptable level.

As Nick approached his car something didn't look right. His wiper blades had been stood up and one had a bit of paper shoved through the gap. Nick got closer and could see there was writing on it. He knew instantly what it was going to be. A note, a message, a threat again from the Irish clan.

Nick picked up the note. It was short and brief.

"We can get to you any time! You're a dead man walking and that won't be for long."

TIME'S UP

That was it. The boss of the family had made his mind up – he was going to kill Nick. The hourglass was filling up slowly, time was running out.

CHAPTER 17

Nick sat in his car and started to daydream and remember that night when he was younger. Bloody hell, that was scary...

Nick got a call from one of the lads, a small crowd he hangs around with, a few from his year and a few from the year below. Apparently, there was some disco down in Apsley at the scout hut. He's wasn't sure about it, although it sounded like it could be a bit of a laugh; even some nice little sorts might be there, he thought to himself.

It was in a scout hut so presumed it would be pretty safe and with decent people; well, at least that's what he thought.

It was on a Friday night. He did not get out that often back then, there was not a lot on for youngsters. Perhaps he should rephrase that: he did go out on Fridays but playing cards at the tennis club is not that exhilarating, plus he'd never meet a girl there. So, he said he'd come along and they arranged to meet nearby at 7.30 p.m. Nick's mate Andy said his dad would give them a lift; his dad was always putting himself out, running them here, running them there. He had a heart of gold and would do anything for anyone.

It was in October and the nights were drawing in; it was

windy and the temperature was falling to zero. As they were dropped, they met up with their other friends, about four or five. Nick and his friends hadn't been there before and Apsley did have a bit of a reputation for having a few unsavoury people up for trouble, people you would cross the street to avoid rather than chance an altercation. However, he couldn't imagine they would be at a scouts' disco.

They walked up a gravel path and there was a patch of water and a mist lingering above; *Bit spooky*, Nick thought to himself. As they entered the hut it looked quite welcoming: dance floor, people hanging around the sides and the odd couple of girls dancing round their handbags. There were a couple of groups of lads here and there, but Nick did not recognise them. He thought, *Is that good or bad?* If there were a few dangerous people he could keep them at a distance or go over to the opposite side.

His first impression was that this was going to be a good, memorable night. It did turn out to be memorable but nearly not good.

After about half an hour more people came in; some he recognised from football and this was a relief to Nick. He was in a local football team back then and tended to know a lot of the faces in Hemel, which was always handy. There were also a few girls he had seen before and would like to know better. He thought maybe this could be the night his luck changed. He was at that awkward age where he was just getting accustomed to drink and its pitfalls; he'd had a few nights getting drunk and did not like the morning-after feeling. Spinning rooms and a banging headache from twelve to two the following afternoon, and added to this it would coincide with his mum nagging him to cut the grass.

On the flip side, he liked getting to the point where he felt a bit merry, and this gave him the confidence to approach some girls and give them a bit of spill. Commonly known as drinking for a bit of Dutch courage.

As Nick and Andy were a year above a few of the other lads in the group, it was up to them to get the drinks and smuggle some to the underage ones of the group.

Nick was heading towards the bar when some guy deliberately barged into him and drink went all over him. He was about to say something when he thought better of it; this guy had that crazy look about him and his little gang looked like trouble. But it was too late; this was the start of a sequence of events that was starting to unravel.

"What you looking at; you want some?" The boy had dark brown hair and raised his arms to his side and swaggered over towards Nick, putting his face within two inches of his.

"No mate, you're all right," Nick said hesitantly, trying to defuse any potential confrontation.

"No, I'm fucking not all right, you prick! You've had it, and your little poofy mates; where you from?" the boy demanded to know with a threatening demeanour.

Nick paused for a minute, probably only ten seconds; options bounced around his head – if he tells the truth then this little gang would know where to find them. On the flip side, they might be scared of where he's from in fear of retaliation, and if that's the case, they could get out unscathed.

"Adeyfield," Nick said proudly. The good thing about coming from Adeyfield was there were some notoriously hard folk and that might make the boy pipe down a bit.

But no, this had the opposite effect.

"Good, I like to kick the fuck out of someone from that area, send a little message of who's who! I think you and your little divvy mates better watch out," the boy said ominously.

Nick got the drinks with Andy and went back to his friends, and told them it was best they all stay together. He told them about his not-so-friendly encounter. He looked over and the boy who had been mouthy had returned to his mates; there looked to be about ten or twelve of them. It was typical of this type of person – the boy was quite small but loud, trying to prove his worth to his crowd. Like a pack of animals, they all became one and they looked over; Nick and his mates were their prey.

This was spiralling out of control, and Nick could not think straight. He surveyed the scene: some girls dancing, cackling about something, a few other groups of lads laughing and drinking, totally oblivious to Nick and his friends' plight.

One of this gang came waltzing over their way. Probably the toughest-looking one of them all, tall, about twenty, chewing gum. He stopped; Nick was awaiting a message. He looked Nick up and down and paused. Then a wry grin formed.

"You! You little cunt, what did you say to my mate?" boy number two said threateningly.

"Nothing, I said nothing!" Nick said nervously, backing away slightly.

"You and your little mates are dead."

They were going to get a right kicking, that was for sure. There was only one exit and he got the impression that this crowd were regulars and knew the surroundings and would close this route off. He was right; within seconds a few of the gang were dispatched to the entrance they had come in from. He contemplated what he was going to do; he felt a little bit responsible for this mess and he wanted to fix it and get them all out unscathed.

"Fuck, Nick, what are we going to do?" Rupert said, a true friend; they had shared many a good time and a laugh, but no run-ins like this was turning into. Rupert was well-educated and had a fantastic sense of humour and could always crack a joke whatever the situation was, but now was not the time. Nick could see a genuine grimace of fear gripping not only Rupert but the whole group.

"I don't know, I don't know." Nick felt his head spinning and it was not drink-related; this time, this was dilemma-related.

A few minutes passed. They stayed strong and together but looks kept coming their way. Tim, one of Nick's mates, came back from the toilet and his nose looked blooded. He looked scared, intimidated.

"What happened?" Keith (one of Nick's friends) said, almost knowingly. "Was that one of them lot?"

"Yes, two of them pushed my head into the wall and then jammed it on to the floor. They said it would be worse later," Tim said, trembling. "I just want to get out of here. Let's go, let's take our chances."

Nick had to do something. These lads looked up to him and even thought he could handle himself, but deep down he knew this crowd were nasty and probably notorious for their area. All of them, including Nick, were out of their comfort zone, out of their depth in a big way.

A few seconds passed. Nick looked around for any escape route, any opportunity to get out of this corner they found themselves in. There had to be a way out.

"We can't go, they've sent some boys to the entrance," Nick said worriedly.

"Let's just tell someone in charge," Rupert said.

Nick thought that was not a bad idea. He mulled that over.

A window of opportunity: Andy Challice just walked in, and Nick knew him. Challice walked over towards the bar, past the Apsley crowd. They seemed to part to each side as Challice walked over, a few nods towards him and a few raised glasses. They all appeared to acknowledge him and respect him, and rightly so. Challice was one of the top boys in Adeyfield and carried a few stories or myths as baggage. Probably hearsay or Chinese whispers but nonetheless he could look after himself.

Nick was not best friends with Challice but knew him well enough to hold a conversation, and they had played football together. What was it with these types of guys? If not being hard and always getting the girls, he was also excellent at football, playing for the district and county when he could be bothered. Nick knew Challice had recently got injured and that was going to be his angle to start a conversation, and start it when the Apsley boys could see.

Nick strolled across the dance floor, trying to play it cool and exude as much confidence as possible. It was however sapping out of his body by the minute; he was scared, but he knew he had to hold himself together for a few moments. It was so important and he had to do a good piece of acting.

Challice had his back to Nick and there were about two rows of people to the bar.

"All right, Andy?" Nick said quite loudly, for two reasons – one, to catch Challice's attention and secondly so the Apsley boys would be aware of his friendship with Challice. As Nick said this, he glanced towards the Apsley boys just for a second. He thought to himself they won't know how well he knew Challice, just some sort of conversation would suffice and bide him and his friends some time.

A few seconds passed. It seemed like an eternity. The Apsley boys were waiting for an outcome. Nick thought, *Oh, Challice, don't blank me, not today.* Challice finally looked round and it all seemed to happen in slow motion.

"Ah, Nick, yeah, mate, how you doing?" Challice said with a smile on his face.

This was perfect, Nick thought. The Apsley boys were about three or four yards away and saw the connection Nick had with Challice. This was panning out just how he had hoped.

"How's your leg, mate; heard you dunnit in a few weeks back?" Nick said confidently and with an air of concern.

"It's a bit sore and stiff, you know, I turned it. Landed funny from jumping up for a header at a corner; be playing in a few weeks. You been up the Chels lately?"

Nick thought this was perfect: he's now holding a conversation with one of the most renowned and feared blokes in Hemel. Having said that, Challice never went looking for trouble, he could just handle it if it came his way. Not many people were silly enough to try it on.

"Yep, went a few weeks ago, West Ham at home," Nick said "Got a bit lively – the ICF came in the Chelsea Shed end – it all kicked off. Bit dicey," Nick continued, relishing his moment.

"Look, Nick, talk to you later; a few babes I gotta see over at the back of the room, you know what I mean," Challice said, hurrying quickly to the area he had just gesticulated to.

"Ah OK, OK. Andy, talk to you later," Nick said, feeling a bit disappointed. It was cut short but the conversation had served its purpose.

It was enough, they were going to be safe. Nick thought it was time to get a few more drinks; he needed something to calm him, although he was buzzing a bit.

He walked over towards his friends, and a hand firmly grasped his shoulder and guided him around in a 180-degree turn.

"You've had a touch; make the most of it. We're watching you. Challice won't be here all night," boy number two said.

Nick got back to the group and explained his little *tête-à-tête* with Challice and reassured them everything was fine whilst Challice was here. Rupert, Keith, Andy and the rest of the boys felt a little bit more relaxed, but this was to be short-lived.

Soft Cell's 'Tainted Love' rang in the background. Nick's favourite. He started to sway back and forth to the music and Marc Almond's distinctive voice coming out of the sound system.

The night got a bit better for about an hour: good music, a few drinks, a laugh etc. It was gone 10 p.m., maybe 10.30 p.m. and Nick had lost touch with what the Apsley boys were doing; he was having a little dance near a nice, cute brunette. She must have been about twenty.

Rupert had learnt that the ringleader was a guy called Kieran and the little cocky bloke who started it all off was called Kobie.

"Nick, is Challice still here?" Rupert said, concerned.

"Yeah, he's over in the back, trying his chances with a few girls," Nick said, a bit jealously.

"Can't see him – are you sure?" Rupert said.

"I'll go and check, ask him if he wants a drink," Nick said reassuringly.

Nick walked over to the back; he could not see Challice, not anywhere. He had gone. This was bad, this was really bad. Challice would not have known that he was their unofficial security. He probably scored with one of those girls. *Damn*, Nick thought to himself.

He was walking back to the lads when he was tripped and pushed to the ground all in one motion.

"Oh, sorry! I think your backup has gone. You're all alone and you're going to get a little beating," boy number two said.

Someone called out to boy number two.

"Kobie, let's leave it," boy number one said.

"No, I won't fucking leave it!" Kobie snapped back.

"Look, don't mess with me or you will live to regret it," Nick said, unconvincingly.

"What, you think Challice will come and take us all on? For

you and your divvy mates? I don't think so. He's gone anyway, with a sort. And you are sort of in trouble with a capital T," smirked Kobie.

Nick was suddenly surrounded by about five to six lads. It was strange; this incident seemed to be in a bubble within this disco – no other people seemed to be aware of the predicament unless they were turning a blind eye in fear of greater ramifications that could include them.

He just about got through the guys, but not before a hard jab to the stomach that nearly had him doubled up. He made his way back to the group and explained Challice had left. Worse than this, the crowd had thinned out, but this Apsley crowd were still there relishing what they were going to do. Nick also told them about his run-in with this Kobie.

"We are in trouble, real trouble. We're going to have to make a run for it, take our chances," Nick said anxiously.

"That's not going to work," Andy said.

"I'm going to call a taxi; in ten minutes we leg it to the top of the street and hop in. If we're lucky we'll get away with it," Nick replied.

"And if we're not?" Andy said, fearing the answer.

"Doesn't bear thinking about – just try and get in a few punches and stick together!" Nick advised.

Nick made the call to the taxi company, and they said there would be one along in ten or fifteen minutes. He gave the precise location for the pick-up and said it was imperative they weren't late.

The time seemed to drag; looks of hatred were being passed

their way, with evil stares, and one lad made a sign of a cut below his neck, side to side. Even the so-called organisers, the scout people, were not to be seen. It was all gathering pace to a conclusion.

"Right, boys, let's go for it," Nick said, directing his words to Rupert.

"Nick, you know we don't think it's your fault – we're just here at the wrong time. If we get out, I'm not coming over this way again, we're just staying with the plums at the tennis club," Rupert joked.

Nick and his friends drifted over to the entrance, but by this time most people had dispersed. Unfortunately, the Apsley lads had spotted their movements and were in close proximity and followed them.

Nick and his friends burst out of the hut.

"Now leg it!" Nick said firmly to them all. They all started to run. Nick was first out of the door. One of the Apsley boys was outside and hit Nick, who managed to push by and shove him to the ground. He could feel the impact of the punch right on the side of his face. He kept running and checked they were all behind him.

They ran down a dirt track that led to the main road. En route was a little pond that had a bit of mist hovering above it. Nick's worst nightmare earlier in the evening was he would end up being thrown in there after a few slaps and kicks from these guys.

The Apsley boys were running close behind, hurling bottles and obscenities at them. Round the corner, up towards the church – and luckily the taxi was waiting.

First part of the getaway was going to plan. The taxi driver must have seen the boys running and knew the gravity of the situation. He pushed open all the doors so they could jump in. It was Nick's uncle John, who was a taxi driver, covering the Hemel area.

Nick and the boys all jumped in and John sped off quickly; a couple of bottles hit and smashed against the windows of the car and Nick's friends just looked at each other in utter dismay. They knew they had got away from a potentially nasty fate.

Needless to say, Nick and his friends never went to any parties out of Leverstock Green and did not go to Apsley for a long time. In fact, Nick recalled it was about a year or so before he ever went back there, to Apsley. He later found out that the gang drank up at the Spotted Bull in Apsley and were a few years older than Nick and his friends.

This episode would probably pale into significance next to what Myles had planned once he got Nick back after ten days.

CHAPTER 18

Nick had this ultimatum hanging round his neck from Myles and the Irish gang and who knew what the next steps were going to be on that front. In fact, he was on the seventh day/ evening of their timescale.

Nick had stopped for a drink on the way home from work, in a lovely country pub; it would have to be quick – he had to get back and sort out his plan of action for his dilemma. The evening was nice and warm and the sun was out, but not dazzling, which Nick liked.

Bill came back with two pints of cider with ice in. They talked about the day's business and the funny events with Jo-Anne and another classic. Nick was telling Bill about something funny that happened yesterday on Bill's day off.

"Jo got all stressed out yesterday; there was an old man with a blind stick but he appeared to be able to see. He was a bit smelly and we were about to close up. It was funny because he was looking at the TVs; Jo-Anne had been doing some price changes but it was home time so she started to turn them off as we do at the end of the day. Anyway, he just moved to the next TV, then the next TV," Nick said, reciting how it played out.

"Oh, what did Jo or say?" Bill said, dying to know the outcome.

"She told the gentleman politely we were closing and he needed to go – plus something like *How can you see you are blind?*" Nick continued.

"To this the man replied, 'I'm visually impaired, I can still see a little – enough to see you put nineteen ninety-nine on that video. Maybe it should be a hundred and ninety-nine, ninety-nine. Goodbye, young lady.' Sure enough, she had put nineteen ninety-nine price on the video, so she was pleased with his feedback."

The beer garden was quite busy as it was a lovely summer's evening. However, there were a few geezers at the top of the garden who looked a bit out of place – overalls on and jumpers. He had noticed them looking over a few times during the evening so far.

Bill and Nick got another drink in and continued to reminisce on some nostalgic stories about the shop and Jo-Anne's classics. Another one was when they convinced her Gotham City was the capital of America.

It looked like this group of blokes was going, so Nick was pleased as they walked past; he felt uneasy as if something was not right with them. They were talking about a football match and results from the previous evening so Nick felt relieved there would be no awkward situation. On first impression they looked the type who liked to start something out of nothing. Just as they got near Nick's table, one paused and looked over. Nick had a sip from his drink and started to pick up the conversation again with Bill.

One of the lads was now walking over to Nick and Bill's table.

"Have you got a light, mate?" he said as he motioned to the cigarette in his hand.

"No, mate, plus I don't smoke. Seriously, it's bad for your health," Nick said, trying to give some advice.

Maybe that was not a good reply, but Nick couldn't help himself. One of the other lads who was leaving joined the conversation and leant into Nick's ear.

"Yeah, you're right, it is bad for your health. So is fucking with the wrong family," he said as he pushed over both nearly-full glasses of drink on to the floor. These smashed in turn and the boys continued to walk out of the garden, sniggering at what they had just done.

Nick was scared; he would need to leave immediately or at the first opportunity.

"Bill, I need to go, mate; forgot I've got to run an errand for my mum tonight," Nick said. Now he was in that place again in his mind about a possible execution and his immediate thoughts were getting back home to his mum and family.

Bill and Nick decided to just stay a few moments while they waited for this white van to go which the lads had all piled into. As the van pulled out of the car park, they beeped the horn continuously and shouted obscenities in the direction of Bill and Nick's table.

Ring-ring. Nick's mobile phone went off; it was a new gadget, and he was quite impressed and about to show off by answering it in the pub garden. He only gave his number to a few people and when he glanced down, no number showed – just *unknown*.

"Hello, who is it?" Nick said loudly so everyone could see he had this mobile phone.

"Time's up!" an Irish voice stated. "We're coming for you very soon; you fucked with the wrong family... it's over."

The line went dead. He thought maybe it was one of those lads who were in the beer garden. Were they just following him and reporting back? One thing that was an absolute: they were on him, on his movements and now on his phone.

"Nick, who was it?" Bill enquired, concerned.

"Mate, nobody. I've got to fly; see you soon," Nick said, in a trance.

Meanwhile at Myles' house, a meeting was going on.

"Seamus, I'm fed up; do take this guy Nick out tomorrow and take Dave from Murphy's family."

"OK, it's not ten days yet," Seamus said; he had not expected the order to be given.

"I don't care – you know what to do and don't fuck up; and it's got to be you!" Myles said assertively.

CHAPTER 19

Nick was driving into work; he was on autopilot, knowing he had to change everything today. The drive was about twenty miles and his mind was racing; they could get to him any time. The snooker incident, the note on his car, the visit at the beer garden. They obviously had people tailing his every move, maybe even this journey. It took him on a few B-roads and he was about four miles from work when he noticed he was being followed, but realistically it probably had been happening from the beginning of his journey.

It could be today he was going to be executed – he had the warning recently from the bogus policemen. It was time to disappear without a trace, tell no one, just head north and hole up in a B and B. He had to wait it out until the police caught Myles and his associates – but would that be the end?

As Nick pulled up outside the back of the shop he noticed Bill was already in, which was a bit strange as he was normally late. Bill had a Capri; it was his pride and joy, immaculately kept with trademark furry dice hanging from the inside mirror. Nick went in, conducted his courtesy *hello*s to his staff and entered the stockroom where his desk was. He stared down at the floor, confused and scared; then Bill came in.

"Nick, you all right? What's wrong?" Bill asked, concerned.

"Nothing, mate, just didn't sleep well last night, a lot on my mind." *Nutty Irish gang*, Nick thought to himself as he replied to Bill.

"Nick, are you holding a staff meeting?" Bill enquired. He looked at Nick and knew something was not right, despite what he had said.

"No, Bill; well, not from me. You do it – who's in?"

"Jo-Anne, Ray and me and you, of course," Bill said.

"I might have to pop out in an hour – got to tune in some old dear's TV," Nick lied. He knew he had to flee today; he was not sure where he was going or when to go. "You do a rallying speech, get them upbeat and positive for the day ahead," Nick said, not totally convincingly.

"OK, will do, no probs," Bill said.

"Soon!" Nick replied.

After about thirty minutes of contemplating, Nick strolled out of the stockroom on to the shop floor. The shop was looking clean and tidy and the staff were nattering about their exploits the night before. If they only knew about his run-in from last night, let alone what had happened a week ago. If any of them thought they had troubles, they paled into insignificance compared to his. Money and girlfriend troubles – that was nothing to having your life threatened.

He wandered to the front door and looked across the road and noticed a car with a couple of men sitting in. It looked like the car that had followed him that morning: a grey, unsuspecting Cortina. He clocked it and the guys, looked up and down the high street as if he hadn't noticed them and headed back into the shop.

It was the Myles gang, no doubt.

The Irish guys sat in the car and as far as they were concerned, Nick had not noticed them. They continued chatting but kept surveillance on the store. They knew or thought Nick would not leave the store, especially as he was manager. They knew everything – when he started and when he finished. They had got their surveillance team up and running very quickly, ever since Myles had given the go-head to tail him everywhere.

A few ladies had slowly walked into the store, rather elderly, wearing thick coats, although the weather was mild. He always thought the elderly wore heavy coats even in the height of summer, looking like they should be at a Sunday church service.

"Going to treat yourself to a Nintendo Sixty-four?" Nick said, jokingly.

"I don't even know what that is, young man. No, we have come to get a new kettle."

"Wow, you're going to make me rich," Nick muttered under his breath, hoping they would not hear properly. He was not his normal self and not normally sarcastic like this to customers.

"What was that?" one of the old ladies said sharply.

"I said we've got a good Richards one – Morphy Richards. Let me get someone to help you part with your money," Nick said politely and with a joke.

The ladies laughed and walked up towards the small appliance section: kettles, irons and general kitchen equipment.

"Jo, can you help these ladies with a kettle; your department, really," Nick said with a subliminal message and joke that women are best in the kitchen.

Nick walked back towards the stockroom. He was going to have to call his boss, Phil, to say he was leaving the shop. Phil was someone he looked up to and did not like doing this, but upsetting his boss in the great scheme of things was the least of his worries.

He picked up the phone and paused for a moment. Maybe he should just call the police with more evidence – these suspicious people outside the shop. Detective Dantry did say to inform him of anything, especially if he felt threatened.

Nick dialled the number and put it on speakerphone. The phone was an all-in-one, fax and answering machine. State of the art for the time. It rang for three to four rings, then a voice.

"Nick, how's it going? Good week last week, a hundred and twenty per cent of our target." Phil greeted Nick's call, presuming it was Nick on the other end. He would be right as no one else from the store would call the boss.

"Yeah, yeah, thanks for that," Nick said, practically dismissing the praise. He had more pressing things on his mind. He was going to quit with no notice; Phil would go mad. He just had to blurt it out.

"Phil, I don't know how I'm going to say this but…" Nick started to say.

Phil was one always trying to second-guess and normally guessing wrong.

"You want some time off? You know you can't; it's a busy period

– you have to give a month's notice. They need you leading from the front; you're one of the top salesmen in the region, despite the fact you should be managing and delegating," Phil said.

"Phil, no, it's not that. Listen to me," Nick said firmly. "I'm going to have to resign. I'm leaving today; now, in fact. I will give the keys to Bill."

"You can't! Don't be silly, you need to give a month's notice," Phil fired back.

"Do I?! Do I really?" Nick said with a touch of sarcasm. He was not in the mood. "You know how you backdate my pay rise, rare may that be? Well, I'm backdating my resignation. I'm off." Nick slammed the phone down.

He then took it off the hook. He knew Phil would go ballistic – no one spoke to him like this, and to be fair, Nick would not dream of it if it was not for his dire situation. He knew Phil would be trying to call back.

Nick was wearing a blue suit. He had to think of a way of disappearing without arousing suspicion. He went to the edge of the shop floor and beckoned Bill into the office.

"Bill, put on my jacket and give me your car keys. Now," Nick said, directly and firmly.

"What's happening? Nick, you're frightening me."

"Listen, I need you to do a big favour for me. I will explain later. I want you to go on the shop floor and use the phone near the till. Pretend to make a call, stay on it for ten minutes, then come out the back for about half an hour. Oh, and keep your back to the front of the shop."

"Why's that?" Bill asked.

"Just… just do it," Nick started to say in a raised voice but managed to curb it at the last moment. Bill had done nothing wrong.

Bill handed his keys to Nick, and Nick exchanged Bill's keys with his own.

"Not bad. You get an up-to-date Golf, I get a dated boy racer Capri with go-faster stripes!" Nick said. "Don't crash it, I will be back for it in a few days, hopefully."

"Nick…" Bill began to say, but Nick was making tracks. There was an exit out of the stockroom to the cars out the back.

Nick had taken some money from the till, about £200. Maybe he could hold out in a hotel somewhere far, far away. As he started up the car, he took down the furry dice, reversed and went out of Ruislip through some back roads.

The Irishmen had orders from Myles: at the end of the day, they would follow Nick and run him off the road, shoot him and bury him in the local quarry. Seamus was in the car. It was just a day in their life; if it wasn't intimidation and racketeering it was causing damage to property, people or cancelling people's lives. They were meticulous down to the last bit of detail – they had to be, the type of work they all did. Mistakes or errors would send any one of them away for years and all the cards would come tumbling down on Myles' empire.

"He's been out the back some while. Dave, you go in and ask for the manager. Make up some story about how your washing machine's gone wrong. Just check he's still there. Don't forget, use your English tongue. Don't raise suspicion – he knows we're out to get him."

"OK, Seamus," Dave said.

Dave got out of the car, looked both ways and trotted across the road. He was dressed fairly casually, his hair a bit bedraggled. He had not bargained for conversation and niceties; as far as he was aware, the day was mapped out. Dave, despite being in Myles' firm for a while, had only done a few hits – shut-downs as they called them. It had been a while since the last – about six months.

Dave looked in the window, then went into the store. He pretended he was interested in the TVs, and soon had the attention of a hungry salesman, Ray.

"Good morning, sir, how are you today?" Ray said politely with a sales plan in his head.

"Look, don't waste your sales pitch on me, I'm actually here to see your boss. Is it Nick?" Dave said knowingly.

"Can I ask regarding what?" Ray said.

"You can, but I won't answer. No, just joking; got a bit of problem with my TV and Nick said to ask for him the next time it went on the blink," Dave continued quite convincingly.

"OK. I'm not sure if he is in. Hold on a minute," Ray said.

Dave was a bit concerned. Had they been given the slip by this Englishman? Had he made a run for it?

Ray went out the back and could not see Nick. He came across Bill in the office.

"Why've you got Nick's suit jacket on?" Ray said, a bit stunned and bemused.

"It's a long story; well, it's not, actually, it's just a story, but you wouldn't believe it – Nick's gone and I don't know when he will be back," Bill replied.

"Gone? Gone where, and why?" Ray said. "How long's he going to be?" he continued.

"Too many questions; just go back on the shop floor," Bill said with a tone to his voice.

Ray trudged out. He didn't like being told what to do, especially from Bill. Bill was two years younger than him, and he felt humiliated; he should be assistant manager. As he got back to the shop floor, he realised he had to go back to the bloke and inform him that Nick was not in. Ray sensed the news would not go down well, and it didn't.

He approached the gentleman, who had his back to him.

"Excuse me, sir, Nick's not actually in," Ray said, still a bit alarmed about the news himself.

"You what? You're fucking joking!" The man had drifted into the Irish accent momentarily.

The Irishman started to walk towards where Ray had come from, thinking maybe Nick was hiding out the back.

"You can't go in there!" Ray said, dropping the *sir*.

"Can't I? You just watch and stay the fuck out of my way if you know what's best, you twat!" Dave shouted.

The Irishman shoved Ray out of the way and entered the stockroom. He was in a raging mood; they had lost their man. Myles was going to go mad when he saw them if they had lost Nick. The stockroom led on to the office where Bill was sitting, contemplating the events of the morning.

The door was thrust open with such velocity the window in the door cracked, with parts falling to the floor. Dave stormed in.

"Where's Nick?!"

Bill just stared; nothing could come out of his mouth. What was happening? No wonder Nick had fled if someone like this was after him, Bill thought.

The Irishman, approximately six feet two in height and about sixteen stone, picked Bill up by his throat and shoved him backwards into a filing cabinet all in one movement. The morning coffee cups fell to the floor and shattered.

Bill was small-framed, could not put up any resistance and for that matter did not want to. His heart was pounding. This was a pretty irate customer; this could not be work-related, no, this had to be something else. No one would act like this if their TV or washing machine wasn't working. *What can Nick have done to have some psycho like this hunting him down?* Bill thought to himself.

"You gonna answer me?" Dave said, by this stage ready to give someone a good hiding.

"I don't know, he had to go out. He'll be back in twenty minutes; do you want to wait?" Bill said, trying to give Nick more time.

"You, you twat, you think I'm stupid? What do you take me for?" he said, raging.

He threw Bill down like a ragdoll, and gave him a kick to the head for good measure. Blood sprayed on to the floor. He ransacked the office, looking for some clue of Nick's whereabouts, then left hurriedly.

He came out of the stockroom and saw that Ray was on the other side of the till, a counter in between them.

"You going to make a call – call the police? I wouldn't if I was you, especially if you value your own and your family's life. Now get the fuck away from the desk, go out the back and stay there!" yelled Dave.

The Irishman went out the only other exit, which led into a kitchen and toilet area. Jo-Anne was there. She had a bit of a nervous disposition and the next few seconds were not going to help that.

He strolled into the area; Jo-Anne dropped a cup and started to shake uncontrollably.

"Where's Nick, you bitch?" Dave screamed, right up in her face.

"Err, err, I-d-d-don't know," Jo-Anne stuttered. She always did this when she was in an awkward situation, which was an understatement.

Dave slapped the woman hard, causing him to damage the flesh on his knuckles. Jo-Anne fell to the floor in a heap. She didn't deserve this; these guys were just ruthless and relentless in pursuit of their cause. She had a bloody nose and started crying.

"You see Nick, tell him we'll find him – and soon." Dave burst back on to the shop floor. "He's a fucking dead man," Dave said.

He fled out of the shop and across the road, nearly getting hit by a car in the process. Once in the car he explained to Seamus that Nick had given them the slip and feared he could be well away in any direction.

"How the hell has that happened? No one came out the front. He must have known we were here; perhaps he clocked us earlier. Myles is going to go fucking mental; we will have to report in that we've lost him. Oh shit," Dave said.

By this time, Nick was a good forty miles away, heading towards the M3. He could book himself in a hotel for a night, then decide what to do. He was going to have to tell the police they were trying to get him again, no choice. He felt sure they would track him down or do something to a family member, even Wayne. They might even know where he lived; Nick was going to have to warn him somehow.

As he drove, his heart was pounding and his head racing with all the different options he had. At least he had got away. He had a little head start, but for how long?

CHAPTER 20

Nick stayed one night in the Farnham area, but decided to go up north, maybe hole up at his aunt's so he could think things through.

As he was driving up, the scenery was flashing by, but it was not registering; he was on autopilot. He hoped his car was not going to give up the ghost or spring an unwanted failure – that was the last thing he needed. He would have to get a message to his mum; she didn't know the danger he was in and he did not want her to have that burden. His brother could have been an option to approach but he would probably have laughed it off and not taken it seriously. Stephen was wrapped up in his world and besotted with his new girlfriend.

Nick noticed a sign for services two miles ahead and decided he would pull off, stretch his legs and get a coffee. As he pulled into the services, he saw a good space to park, near a little picnic bench, with a small grassed area. Perfect, go to the toilet, get a coffee and chill for forty minutes or so and watch the world go by.

He sat down and thought about the predicament he was in. He'd had some unwanted run-ins before, and the sign to

Manchester had set off another memory from just two years earlier.

He went to a football match, Manchester United versus Chelsea, and he went from London on one of those beaten-up "special" (not-so-special) trains. London Transport had designated trains reserved for notorious football teams, the likes of West Ham, Millwall and Chelsea. He was with his familiar friends, Andy, Alan and Jonathan, who all went to the Chelsea games together. Now they weren't hooligans as such, but enjoyed being on the periphery of that scene and singing the songs; that was as far as they wanted to go. Normally that was all that would happen, then they would spin a yarn about this or that scrape to make them sound in with the top boys. It was funny, really, looking back.

Not that day, though. The train turned up at Manchester Picadilly station. They were herded out as normal into a police escort and then that would take you up to the ground. There would be hurls of abusive language and the Chelsea boys would give it back. The well-known so-called *top boys* would be itching to escape the escort and get into a fight but Nick wanted no such incident happening to him or his friends.

That day they were being bundled along, nearly floating as the crowd took them with it. All of a sudden, about twenty lads broke free and out of the police ring (which was meant to stop both sets fighting each other) into the waiting Manchester fans who were lining the roads. It would be the norm for bottles and bricks to be thrown. Nick found himself swept along and outside the police cordon with Alan as well. They looked at each other, petrified, as they would have to fend for themselves and possibly even start fighting. It was a blur, difficult to tell who was on which side.

Nick threw a few punches at some lads, also receiving a few back and some kicks thrown in for good measure. It was so scary; he didn't know if he would get beaten half to death with kick after kick; and if he went down there was no chance of getting back up, game over.

It must have been about two minutes – it seemed like half an hour – but somehow some policeman managed to get a few of them out, including Alan and himself. He went to the match and Chelsea lost, nothing new back in that era, but the whole time he thought about what could have happened and always remembered how lucky he was.

What with this and the Apsley incident, he thought he'd had a charmed existence so far, as if someone was looking over him. On recollection good memories despite the fear at the time. He was not so sure how this Irish gang and rape allegation was going to playout – hopefully he'd be guided through from a more powerful existence.

He drank his coffee and continued his journey, and about an hour later he arrived at his aunt's. He could hole up here and, as he would famously say to his friends when there were problems, "it will sort itself out". He hoped so.

His aunt made him tea and gave him some home-made cake. Later he went to bed, wondering what the next day would have in store for him.

CHAPTER 21

The McGinley family were gathered at the mansion for a meal. Terry and Jack were up from London, and a few other gang members from Manchester and Glasgow were there as well. Myles was conducting a meeting about proposed plans in the future and updates on recent jobs, hits and even good old-fashioned bank/post office heists.

Generally, Myles was pleased with the operation but was concerned about the recent fracas with Seamus and himself at the gents' club a few weeks earlier. The recent bank job had gone perfectly and netted them upwards of £300,000.

Despite the house taking on the appearance of a stately home, there was state-of-the-art technology in most rooms: CCTV surveillance, security training and schooling for elocution to name just a few. Myles even had a close family member studying law, finance and stocks and shares. His medium-term plan was to go legitimate and stop the illegal activity or make it very minimal. Myles had promised Judith he would get them away from this and retire with a place in the south of France and a nice cottage in a village close to Belfast, their heritage and origin.

He knew it was going to take a while and he had some unfinished business that included a few hits on rival gangs. It was the only way and option once you got so far up in the underworld chain of organised crime. The McGinley family was infamous now amongst rival gangs and many tales were told of the jobs they had carried out. It had even got to a stage where rival gangs and drug dealers would seek their protection or ask them to execute jobs for their gangs at a price. So, the McGinley syndicate would take a commission for a job. Sometimes they would not even be involved in the score, just allow or authorise a gang to carry it out and they would take a levy from it.

The household was discussing jobs, money and agendas for the coming weeks. Judith kept them all refreshed with tea and cakes. As the evening wore on, they went on to the stronger liquids like JD and Cokes and Guinness. Eileen was milling about helping her mum, watching TV and making a few calls from her room to her latest boyfriend. (She would keep this secret from her dad.)

"Dad, we have the whereabouts of Nick – we followed him up north. He's holing up at his aunt's; what do you want to do? We won't cock up again," Seamus said.

"OK, we have a family up there on a large estate with a helipad. I will give the nod to get him shortly. Keep me updated and if movements change, let me know. I just want him back at our place; I don't want the hit done out in public – too risky. I want to hear him beg for mercy!" Myles said, staring through people. He wanted retribution.

Myles contacted the O'Reilly family up north and spoke to the eldest brother who ran the outfit since his father's stroke. He said he needed a favour done; a lad to be picked up and brought down, and to use the helicopter they had. Myles stressed that he wasn't to be hurt and no noise should be made up north – just bring him down with no fuss.

The son said it would be their pleasure to assist the McGinley family. Myles gave him the name and description, plus the address that Seamus had given him. He indicated it would be in the next few days and to be ready at short notice.

CHAPTER 22

Dantry had called a meeting for an update on the McGinleys' activities, and there had been some interesting developments. Scrivener and Cook were present and a colleague from the Herts police as well. They had built up a profile of the key people within the organisation.

Dantry started the meeting off with every detail, an outline of what they knew and information that had come to light in the last few weeks. The McGinleys' work was also being watched by some members of MI5 because of Myles' link to the IRA, and they would sometimes attend briefings. Dantry had to send all evidence and findings regarding Myles McGinley and his family's activities to MI5. Dantry was a stickler, almost OCD on how he ran his investigations, and he got infuriated if his team members did not practise the same attention to detail.

"OK, there is a file on the server of what I'm about to say but I thought I would talk it through to give you an overview of the McGinley gang, known associates and recent information gained. So, we know Myles and Patrick are the leaders and they go back to paramilitary activity in Belfast and operations for the IRA on mainland Britain as well. There are two other key members, believed to be Jack, who heads up the London division of 'The Outfit' and a guy called Simon who is a trouble-shooter, literally, so to speak, and very aptly nicknamed by my PA. Added to this we have Seamus who is heavily involved. He is a loud-mouthed drunk whom Myles has issues with. We have a couple of incidents involving Seamus shouting his mouth off and letting things slip things during drunken binges. I will come to this a bit later. Coming back to the family, there is a daughter, Eileen, who is involved in some bits, and the wife, Judith, who once again is involved in low-level ops, mainly organisation. Lastly, Conor, the youngest son, but as far as we know and as discussed in our last meeting, he stays in the house," Dantry said.

Dantry passed over to Scrivener to give an update on recent findings.

"Thank you, sir. So, recent activity and initial evidence has been compiled. Firstly, Seamus' incident at the gents' club. We did get some statements from the security of the venue plus evidence from an undercover cop. The security guy that night states hearing Seamus threatening and hitting an individual, saying you should not mess with their family or words to that effect. Off the back of this, we set up surveillance and planted a bug on their favourite reserved table. It took a week before Myles and Seamus came back; we had an undercover cop disguised as a waitress, plus plain-clothed policemen posing as customers at the venue. The outcome was a recorded conversation where Myles makes an admission of the threat on the young man, Nick, and says he will need to shut him up for good. Later in the conversation there is dialogue about a hit on a young boy in a London nightclub. This was looked into and we noticed Jack, one of Myles' top boys, was the brains behind this hit. At present, local police think it was a disagreement between two rival gangs. We have now passed over information to the local force investigating this murder and are very close to developments."

Dantry then concluded the meeting. "With the cooperation of Sergeant Stewart from the Hertfordshire police, we have interviewed this Nick Scott about his kidnap by Myles. Scott was initially blindfolded but when presented to Myles, it was removed. He was accused of raping his daughter and was given ten days before they would kill him or one of his family members. We are not sure of the significance of the ten-day period; maybe he wants to make him sweat or think about how he will kill and dispose of this guy." Dantry continued. "This Nick Scott gave an accurate description and it's definitely Myles McGinley, so we have another two charges added to Myles' rap sheet of kidnap and threat to murder, plus the hit in London. We will have to pull out this Nick witness and put him in a safe house as soon as possible. As mentioned at the top of the brief, Seamus was caught at a casino mouthing off again and allegedly talking about a drug deal they pulled off. This was faintly picked up on a planted bug, but we think the quality is good enough to use in court. So, well done, team, we are making progress."

The officers all dispersed and went about their daily duties.

CHAPTER 23

Nick knew his excursion up north could only be temporary, and that he was putting more people at risk, namely, his dear aunt. Although it was nice seeing and staying with her it was inappropriate and bad timing. Detective Dantry had indicated that he shouldn't move about, but the Irish turning up at the shop made him panic and flee. Now, on reflection, he should have sought sanctuary by going straight to the police station. However, he had the dilemma of what they might do to his dear nephew who was only two years old.

Nick got up early, did a few chores around the house for his aunt, had a cup of tea and spoke about what was going on in the world. He did not burden his Aunt Sue with any of his problems; she had her own, like arthritis in the knee and hip. He felt good as he cut the grass front and back, and also got a few groceries from a local corner store. His thoughts were constantly on what Myles was going to do, and that he had not had a good night's sleep since the kidnap, and what the significance was of the ten days. Maybe if caught, and face to face with Myles, he should admit to rape – that might be the best course of action.

Later that day he called his mum just to check she was all right and to let her know he was fine.

"Mum, how are you? Everything OK down there?" Nick asked.

"Yes, good. Where are you? You flit in and out of the house as if it's a hotel. It's not good enough! Your work has rung wondering where you are. I didn't know what to say," his mum replied.

"Oh, don't worry about work; I'm giving that up. I don't like the company any more – too demanding in some areas and not appreciative at all," Nick went on. "Anything untoward happened to you? Any strangers coming to the door or hanging around?"

"No. Actually, yes; we did have a call from a Detective Dantry asking where you are and leaving his number for you to call ASAP," his mum said. She gave him the number.

Nick thought Mum's memory was going – surely this would have been the first thing she would have said?

"Oh, we also had the rag and bone man call; never seen him before. He asked if we had any tat to clear, but also asked for you by name. I thought this was strange; how would he have your name?"

Nick happened to agree with his mum's anxiety about this. They were all over him like an unwelcome rash.

"OK. Mum, don't worry about that. I've got to go, I'll see you soon," Nick replied, then hung up.

Armed with that information and the unwelcome visit to his mum's address, he decided to call Detective Dantry. It was too coincidental. That trade was normally done by the Irish and he couldn't remember the last time one of them came round;

he would have been aged ten or so. This gang was closing in and had all avenues covered, it seemed.

Nick punched out the numbers on his aunt's phone.

"Detective Dantry, how can I help you?" Dantry said in an authoritative voice.

"Hi, it's Nick Scott. I've gone up north, but I believe the Irish family are stepping up and trying to get me. They came to my shop the other day and, I think, with the intention of taking me," Nick said nervously.

"OK, calm down, they can't know your location up there. To be brutally honest, we have got wind they are coming for you. Some other info has come to light and this is a violent crime syndicate you have been drawn into. I need to ask you to do something. It is dangerous but it will bring this to closure; you will be able to go back to your life and we can get more evidence to convict Myles and the rest involved."

Nick hesitated, then replied, "OK, just let me know what you want me to do. Can you send someone to keep an eye on my mum's house? I believe part of his crowd were there yesterday posing as rag-and-bone collectors." Nick was very concerned about his family.

"Yes, we will dispatch someone in an unmarked car to monitor, protect your mum and hopefully get a lead on the whereabouts of the house to which you were taken," Dantry said. "So, this is what I need you to do. You say you're near Manchester. I want you to go to a police station in Altrincham; they will fit a bug on you that gives off a location of where you are. After that I suggest you come back down south, come to the police station, then we will provide a safe place for you until this is sorted," the detective concluded. He gave him the name and address of who to see at the station.

About an hour later Nick drove to the address of the police station in Altrincham. He was there about two hours with the contact Dantry had given. They fitted the small device, the size of a five-pence piece, on the top part of his chest. Nick then returned to his aunt's. He would head down to his mum's the next day. Finally this nightmare might be over.

CHAPTER 24

Daniel, Myles' cousin, was going to a club up west with a couple of friends, Mark and Dave. It was a hip-hop-type club and they loved the music and vibe, and the girls in short dresses. It was a predominantly Afro-Caribbean mix but it also had white people frequently trying out their dance moves.

The boys arrived at the club; there was a small queue and about ten groups. It was about 10 p.m. – that was the time the regulars would go there. Daniel and his friends had already had a few drinks at a local pub in Streatham and got to the club via the bus.

"Hold on," the bouncer said to them. "You been here before?"

"Yes," Daniel said, as if they were almost regulars.

"Well, you know the rules – no drugs or fighting and watch out for some of the gangs in here."

They entered the club. Despite Daniel being connected to a notorious gang, he did not want to get in any trouble or for that matter, see his good friends in trouble. They had all grown up together and were close. Mark and Dave knew Daniel was related to some unsavoury people, but Daniel was not involved in that business. Daniel thought you cannot choose your family but they were handy to call upon if trouble ever flared up.

The music was loud and they couldn't hear each other now. The bouncer was correct – there were little pockets of gangs spread around the club, some white kids but the majority were ethnic. Daniel and his friends walked towards the bar, they could feel their gazes on them and some people were staring them out. They just kept their heads down and avoided eye contact.

Some pretty girls at the bar, Daniel thought. "Oh, barman, you serving?" Daniel said in his thick Irish accent.

"Yes; what you having, Paddy?" the barman joked.

"Ha ha, you're funny. I'll have three pints of Castlemaine," Daniel said.

The barman poured the drinks and they walked deeper into the club. It was cool; over three floors with different DJs playing all varieties of music, hip-hop, house and soul.

They decided to go up to the second floor as they liked the music the DJ played. As Daniel was walking up a guy brushed against him on the stairs. He thought nothing of it; it was a faint touch.

"Watch where you're going, you jerk," the boy said.

The boy was tall about six feet two with West Indian heritage; *late teens or early twenties*, Daniel thought to himself.

"Sorry," Daniel said.

"Yeah, you will be! Do you know who I am?" the boy said. "Oh, fuck it, I can't be bothered with you; just fucking stay out of my sight."

Daniel took his advice and continued up to the second floor. The boys soon forgot about the incident and were enjoying the music, had a few too many drinks and were watching the girls dancing sexily.

"Mark, you go up and throw some moves; you can always get chatting with the ladies," Daniel said.

"OK, take some notes for another time," Mark said cockily.

The boys continued to have a good night. They didn't get far with the ladies but had some good dances and the music was banging. A few drinks, chats about previous exploits and a bit of football talk and general banter between them all.

The night wore on and they were starting to feel very delicate, so decided it was time to go. They didn't want to wait to the end as that's when trouble could happen.

"Mark, I've just got to go to the toilet, then we'll shoot off," Daniel said.

The toilet was on the first floor. He had been down about an hour before and luckily hadn't bumped into any shady characters, and in particular the boy from the beginning of the evening. The stairs were narrow and filled with disco smoke that swirled around and made it very difficult to navigate anywhere.

There were neon lights that said GENTS ahead so Daniel was there with no encounters – good. He thought, *OK, toilet and be back home about one a.m. – won't feel too bad for tomorrow.* He had to go out with his dad to pick up some pallets; their family was legitimate and had nothing to do with Myles' untoward activities. They had been asked by Myles to participate in some low-level jobs but Daniel's dad was adamant he did not want anything to do with it or them.

Daniel approached the door and a couple of guys fell out, obviously very drunk. It was that time of night where the excess alcohol started to kick in.

He went up to the urinal. A few seconds later about six black boys came in. Two went to the urinals either side of Daniel.

"Hey, you fucking prat, watch what you're doing," one said. The boy recognised Daniel from earlier in the night. "You just knocked into me; do you rate yourself, then?" the boy said. "You again, this is twice tonight you have pissed me off."

"Look, I'm sorry, I'm not looking for trouble," Daniel said, even though he didn't feel he had touched the boy.

"What you got on you? Give me your money and that watch and that chain," the boy insisted.

From nowhere, a crack to his side from one of the other boys. Daniel dropped to his knees. A kick to his stomach then to his head, one boy spat on him and the others laughed as they rained punch after punch.

"Stop!" screamed Daniel.

"Here's a souvenir." The boy stuffed a business-type card in his mouth and then thrust Daniel to the ground again.

"It's Abs from the LJC crew of ninety-two," he sniggered as he beckoned his boys out of the toilets.

Daniel looked up. The room was spinning from the alcohol intake and kicking he'd taken; not a good combination. He managed to spit out a few words before falling unconscious. "Bad move, you..." Daniel didn't finish his sentence, and slumped in a pool of his blood.

"Oh, shut the fuck up you div. If I see you in here again, I'll cut you." Abs left the toilets swiftly with his boys.

CHAPTER 25

"So, you know the boy's name. Send some people down to the neighbourhood. I want this sorted quickly; no one turns over one of our boys. Bloody foreigners, think they can come over to our country and take over. Sort it," Myles cursed to the room.

"Well, technically it's not our country, but I know what you mean," Patrick said sarcastically.

Myles gave him one of his looks as if to say *This is not funny* or rather, *not the time*. Patrick realised this and gave a look back saying sorry. It was not a laughing matter. They had known each other for years and sometimes words were not needed.

"Yes, Myles, will do; come on Simon," Patrick said.

Simon was one of the family's close friends, loyal to the bone and ruthless at carrying hits through. He knew this manor well and had connections.

"Patrick, this boy is a dead man walking," Simon said, fuming at what happened to Myles' cousin.

Simon went down to Peckham with about three men for the job. He had a few Jamaicans who were on the payroll and able to find out where this *Abs* was. They would fit in and not raise suspicion and they were very good at getting information.

As like many of the Jamaicans: gift of the gab, and they could sweet-talk most of the ladies as well.

His boys, Winston and Eddy, went into a few youth clubs but couldn't seem to track the boy down. One lad thought he had heard of this boy playing football for one of the local teams.

Winston had a lead, an angle, a foot in the door; that was all he needed. They went to the local pub, normally the hub of most towns, a starting place for gossip and what's going on in the street.

"Hi, yes, I've just moved into the area and my boy wants to join a football team. Do you know who I can talk to about it?" Eddy enquired in a meaningful manner.

"If you go to Sheep Lane on Sunday morning, there are three to four teams. Just talk to one of the mums or dads – they'll point you in the direction of the manager."

Eddy went away and gave Patrick an update that he thought he could be close to the boy and would have more news on Sunday afternoon.

"That's good stuff, Eddy; get this little cunt as soon as poss. Talk to you later," Patrick said.

Eddy went down on Sunday, and there were about eleven or twelve pitches and lots of games going on, hundreds of kids and know-it-all parents effing and blinding on the touchlines; it was hard to believe. They were only kids' matches but seemed more like life or death for some of the parents, and the mums were the worst. Eddy wasn't getting anywhere and he was starting to think he would have to try another way of tracking down this Abs boy.

Eddy went up and down the touchlines of the pitches. There were lots of teams built up of predominantly black kids. It was good that they were channelling their energy to this rather than gang culture. Eddy, as a kid, had hung around with the wrong crowd and hadn't tried hard at school; the few times he went in were only for sports lessons. Now with no qualifications, he found himself racketeering, minding and offering protection for some gangster Irish family and the occasional hit/execution.

He wondered for a moment or two how he had ended up there, hunting down one of his own. He should have pursued his love for sports; maybe become a coach or sports teacher.

Maybe he should call it off, give it up, get out of this living nightmare he found himself in. He couldn't, though; he was in Myles' pocket. He'd done things for him, maimed a few people, leaving them incapacitated, and worse than that he'd cancelled people's contracts – their lives.

Eddy was just making his way back to the car when he came across another game. He watched for a while. They were good, pacey and clinical finishers, streets ahead of any other teams on the pitches. Eddy knew a bit about football; he'd reached a semi-professional standard in his younger days, so could pass judgement and could have played the part as a football scout had his life panned out differently.

Eddy paused for a moment, considering what could have been. He was a good motivator, and could have nurtured and encouraged talent. Never mind. Now, instead, he was on verge of orchestrating a hit on a teenager.

"Corner, ref!" screamed one young lad towards the referee.

To be fair he was right, and the ref signalled over to the lad: corner.

One of the lads went over to take it, when there was a loud shout from one of the boys at the back. "Hold on, I'm going up. My head's gonna get on the end of it, and let Abs take it."

Eddy heard this and he stopped dead in his tracks. This could be the lad he was after. The boy was a big lad for his age, maybe sixteen or seventeen years old. He looked pretty sure of himself as he trotted over, picked the ball up and ran over to the quadrant. He put his hands up; this normally signalled maybe near-post or back-post delivery.

Eddy watched the rest of the game; the boy was an excellent prospect and extremely skilful for his age. He was convinced this was the boy who did Myles' cousin in at the club. He waited patiently until the game was finished. The match was one-sided in the end and the Black Panthers, as they were called, had won quite convincingly, 5-0, and Abs had scored twice.

The team gathered round in a huddle and the manager (Eddy presumed) commended them all on their performance. The manager called Abs forward and gave him a little trophy, probably 'man of the match'. He was pleased. Eddy was sickened at the thought of what he was going to do if this was indeed the boy in question. He seemed so normal, playing football with his friends – was he really the same lad that had kicked the Irish boy to within an inch of his death? Why the hell had he done such a callous thing?

Eddy didn't really want to follow it through, but he knew he had to. He breezed over to the bunch and butted in on the conversation.

"Lads, that was a cracking match, some great performances," he said. "Let me introduce myself. I'm Harry Wright and I do a bit of scouting for a few teams. I'm looking for a few players to have trials at Fulham."

"Fulham?" a couple of lads repeated back to him and glanced to and fro at each other, very pleased, impressed and hopeful.

"Bloody hell, man; any of us you like the look of, mister?"

"Pity it's not the Chels," one lad perked up.

"Better than nobody!" exclaimed another.

"Yeah, your number ten, who's that?" Eddy enquired, even though he knew the lad's name or nickname.

Abs stepped forward and Eddy shook his hand, took him to one side and had a little chat. After about five minutes he arranged to meet the boy and his parents the following Tuesday evening.

Eddy gave an update to Myles to say he thought he had found the teenager in question, and was finding out more on Tuesday.

Tuesday evening came round and Eddy turned up at the boy's house. His purpose was to get evidence that this was the perpetrator of the beating. He started out with the formalities of what it meant to be a professional or apprentice at a top premier club. He sold and painted a grand picture of fortune and fame to the boy and his family. Eddy went on about dedication and determination, the sacrifices that had to be made, etc.

After approximately half an hour he asked the parents if he could go for a little walk with Abs to get to know a bit more about him.

Abs got his coat and they went for a stroll near the boy's house. After a few minutes of small talk, like where he went to school, which team he supported etc., Eddy angled the conversation in the direction he wanted, hopefully to get the confession or admission he was after. He had to force the conversation; his boss wanted immediate results and he had to take a gamble to extract the info he wanted.

"Abs, if you are going to be an apprentice at Fulham you have to conduct yourself correctly, not just on the field but when you're off it as well. Too much for one so young can be the downfall of any up-and-coming footballer. Many a precocious talent has pissed it all down the drain, do you get what I'm saying? It's sometimes over before it gets started," Eddy said, hopefully getting the boy to let down his guard inch by inch.

"Yes, Harry, I fully understand. I would be totally committed and bust my gut to become a professional; that's all I have ever dreamed of since I was a five-year-old. Whatever you or the club people say, I would follow. Look, mister, give me a chance. I would be totally focused, zoned in – I would practise and practise. I need this break. You would see me after every training session doing more, doing corners, free kicks, dribbling skills; you'd have to drag me off the pitch," Abs said convincingly.

"That's good to hear. That's what we want from any apprentice; not all make it, it's a tough learning curve with lots of cheap talent coming from overseas, keeping our youth out. You've got to give a hundred per cent: no late nights, drinking and partying, catch my drift? It's a once-in-a-lifetime opportunity."

Eddy was really laying it on thick; he even convinced himself he was a scout.

"What do you do in your spare time – go to clubs, drinking, chase the ladies? I can bet you're a bit of a ladies' man. Love and leave them type, eh?!"

"Well, I go out with my mates, we have a few drinks, and yes, I do all right with the young girls. They like me, if you know what I mean."

"There's a local night club, what is it, Brown's? Do you go there? I hear it's a happening place with the youngsters round here," Eddy continued.

A few more questions and hopefully he would get the facts and his confession and the green light to finish this boy's life. It was not what Eddy wished for – he wanted to tell the boy to move on and leave the area. Revenge or retribution for most gangs would suffice; it would just be a good hiding, roughed up with a few bruises. But with the McGinleys it was game over, execution. No trail, no evidence, no witnesses. Ruthless.

It would be no good, though. Myles didn't leave unfinished business. He liked to be meticulous, no stone unturned, no loose ends and no comeback to the firm. This potential hit was small fry compared to what the Irish family had been involved in, and Eddy had been part of that on other jobs. There was only going to be one outcome and it would mean this young boy's life going before he could fulfil his potential. He probably could have been a professional; a lot could, but they don't get seen.

"Yeah, I hang out at Brown's all the time, me and my boys go down there every Friday. Normally there's some fit babes there," Abs said with a cheeky smile and a glint in his eye, saying indirectly he'd had a few successful scores there with the ladies.

"Youngsters' place. Is it mainly Afro-Caribbean lads who go there?" Eddy enquired, leading Abs down a dead-end alley where he was about to hang himself, metaphorically, that is.

"Mainly blacks and homies, but you do get a few anaemic people. We normally deal with them, make them feel unwelcome," Abs bragged.

Eddy thought this unfortunately confirmed the type of boy Abs was. He was going to ask the lad outright.

"I hear a young Irish boy got done over pretty bad, Abs; I heard it was you. I've had to do a bit of background on you, if you're coming to Fulham Football Club. Obviously, subject to a good, well, outstanding trial."

Eddy put the feelers out; what reaction was he going to get? Maybe it wasn't the lad, maybe he wouldn't admit it, fearing to jeopardise his trial.

"No, mister, that weren't me. I heard about it, though," Abs said, not so convincingly.

This was a sign. Eddy could sense the boy was lying; his lure of gold would hang him.

"Look, Abs, if you want a chance at the big time, you have got to be honest, you've got to be truthful, transparent. I know it was you."

"OK, OK it was me. I was with the lads and I just got carried away, showing off," Abs said worriedly, fearing this was the end of his dream before it had even started.

"Look, I'm glad you've been honest. Don't worry, but I do want you to put it right and do the right thing, the honourable thing. Go to that club in a fortnight, say sorry, and give the lad fifty pounds." Eddy told Abs it was not up for discussion.

"I will have someone watching, someone your age who will report back to me. You OK with that?" Eddy said sternly.

"Where am I going to get that kind of money?"

"You'll find it somehow. Blag it off somebody. Once you've done that, I will be in contact with you and your family and we will arrange the trial, OK? I'm off now. Not a word to your folks about this misdemeanour; you have to put it right, though. I mean it – keep this between us. Be in touch," Eddy finished.

He then casually walked off into the evening sunset, glancing back at Abs. He was probably daydreaming of stardom, fast cars and scantily clad women chasing him.

Eddy quickened his walk; he had to put things in place and he had to execute this with the utmost precision. Abs was such a young boy. He had just picked on the wrong lad, and his fate had taken him into the path of the McGinley family.

Eddy was sick inside about his next course of action. Firstly, he had to make contact with Myles and Patrick to say he had located and got a confession from the lad. When Myles received this information there would only be one order, one outcome. Abs would be dead.

Eddy would call from a landline phone box. Although mobile phones were just becoming available, the Irish firm still weren't convinced. They thought they could be hacked into to locate the whereabouts of the user, thus maybe revealing their headquarters and dwelling. Where possible, no unnecessary risk was taken.

Eddy saw a telephone box. He opened it up and stepped inside; there was some graffiti and a stale smell of urine; a couple of condoms for good measure as well.

"Hello, is that you, Eileen? Is your dad about?" Eddy said, shaking a bit. "It's Eddy."

"Hold on, I'll transfer you; I think he's in the games room. What are you up to?" Eileen said, being nosey as usual.

"Nothing much, this and that, just putting a few wagers down for your dad. Don't tell your mum, though."

"Dad, I got Eddy on the line; you free?" Eileen said.

"Yeah, yeah, put him through to my room in about thirty seconds."

Myles rushed up a level from his games room to his office, to privacy and comfortable surroundings. Hopefully this was the news he had been waiting for; this cocky dude had been found.

"Eddy! Hope this is good news," Myles said firmly down the phone. "Hold on, I'm just going to pour myself a large cognac, and you're going to tell me you've found this bastard."

A few seconds passed and Eddy gathered himself. He thought the news he had should cheer Myles and Patrick up; they didn't like any loose ends. No unfinished business, and most of all, no one, no one, picked on his friends and family and got away with it.

"Eddy, you there? Give me a quick update of what you've found down in London," Myles said.

Eddy proceeded to go through events step by step and left

no detail out. Myles wanted every last grain of information. He could tell by Myles' occasional feedback and quiet periods that he was pleased with Eddy's work and thoroughness. Eddy told Myles who would carry out hit – an old friend of his in London that owed him.

"Eddy, that's great work. You know what to do now – kill that fucker," Myles said menacingly into the phone. "As discussed the other week, you have all the info, the private aircraft, the pilot, the runway stretch, the safe house and the money. You said you would be using Stephen Richards from London who used to work for us. Don't, I repeat, don't fuck up!"

"Myles, you know you can count on me," Eddy said reassuringly.

"I know – that's why I gave you the job." Myles laughed down the phone.

Eddy stepped out of the phone box. How could he be part of this, killing a young lad? Scarring a family for life with the loss of their son. Eddy thought he could get out, go incognito. Just for a moment, he could see a happier ending for him and Abs. It would not work, though – he would be found, Myles would kill him, his family; too much to lose. Plus Myles would still find Abs, and the outcome would be the same.

During Eddy's stay down in London, he looked up some old friends. One went back a long way; he'd been with the firm in the early days but had stepped away. He was a friend he used to do weights with many years ago and who owed him a no-holds-barred favour. He had already sounded out a few days earlier the job he had for him and the pay he would get. It had been arranged, and his old friend Stephen Richards had a son of a similar age to Abs.

He went to Stephen's house one evening. He told Stephen his son had to do the hit on Abs. Stephen tried to insist he would not do it, but he knew of Eddy's current background and the Irish gang from old.

Eddy told Stephen to come out of the house as he did not want to shout with his family in earshot, and they went for a walk down a nearby street.

"Right, you got it? I want your son down Brown's, Friday the twelfth. I will meet him and give him the gun."

"Eddy, please?" Stephen pleaded with him. "I don't want me or my son to be part of this. I'll go to the police," he said, and started to walk away.

Eddy bundled Stephen across the road into a nearby park. Eddy got him with a grasp round the back of the neck, and a second later, Stephen's nose was in the grit and a gun was at the side of his head.

"You will fucking do as I say, you hear me? Don't push it!" Eddy said quietly but assuredly into Stephen's ear.

He pushed his face forcefully into the ground, grazing his cheek and blood began to flow. He picked up his head by his ear and banged it into the ground a couple of times for good measure. Eddy had been a boxer when he was younger, and had had many a scrape – that was why he was on the McGinley payroll.

"OK, OK, sorry, Ed; stop it!" Stephen stuttered back.

Eddy moved on, but not before whispering in Stephen's ear,

"I know where you live. I know your daughter's nursery and I know your mum's care home; do I make myself crystal?!"

"Yes."

"Good!" Eddy concluded.

THAT FRIDAY-BROWN'S, PECKHAM

Eddy was parked up in a blacked-out Range Rover with tinted windows. Queues were forming outside the club; it was approximately 8 p.m. Crowd and party revellers were there, probably seventy per cent Afro-Caribbean, then the rest were white dudes, wannabe black people born in the wrong skin.

Eddy could overhear the conversations and the white lads were trying their hardest to sound down with their homies. Girls were dolled up in high heels and short skirts; if only their mothers knew where they were.

Eddy's mind had wandered – he had to get back with it and the job in hand. Daniel, the Irish teen who had been done over. was not there; in fact, he had been told by Myles never to frequent Brown's again.

Eddy peered out the window and saw Stephen's son George coming across. As planned, he was wearing a large trench coat to conceal the gun. Eddy nodded for the lad to get in the passenger side. The boy opened the door and jumped into the 4 x 4. He looked petrified and was shaking; he was just a boy thrust into a man's world. Eddy had paid off the doormen to let Stephen in, no questions. Amazing what people will do for £500.

"Calm down and pull yourself together," Eddy said firmly. "Now your dad told you what you need to do and the fall-out if you don't follow what I say."

"Yes," the scared boy said, looking into Eddy's eyes.

"Good, now do you know this Abs guy; will he recognise you?"

"I only know him to nod or say all right to," George replied.

"Ideal. Here's the shooter, this is how you take the safety catch off. Have it poised and ready to go. Don't blow your legs off. Remember, don't be conspicuous and don't draw any attention to yourself. If possible, do it when he goes to the toilet – there'll be fewer people around. It has a silencer on to reduce noise. I will have some people posing as security; they will get you in and out the club and they will follow you. Make sure you don't have a change of heart. They will get you out when the deed is done, all right?"

"Is there any other way?" asked George.

"I'm sorry, no. Your dad had a big debt hanging over him and he has to rebalance it, end of, no more questions. Right, off you trot; I'll see you later tonight."

The boy went and joined up with his friends in the queue. Eddy's Range Rover slowly left and was soon gone. He parked up nearby and was on walkie-talkie contact with one of his men inside.

George (Stephen's son) was soon in the club, and it was heaving. His mind and head were spinning, and he felt claustrophobic. This was big; taking someone's life who he did not know, who had done him no wrong. His heartbeat began to race threefold, sweat seemed to form across his brow and yet he felt cold and sick all at the same time. His friends were talking to him but his mind was miles away; he felt he was outside, looking in on life from above. Even at a young age George had known right from wrong.

Eddy sat in the 4 x 4 at the back of the club. He had notified Myles that the episode involving Abs would be finished and concluded tonight. Eddy, with Simon's help, had also arranged that George, Stephen and the new girlfriend would all be taken away to Scotland to start a new life with a sweetener of fifty thousand pounds to get them up and running. Simon tended to do a lot of ID and forgeries for the McGinleys – this was why he was on this particular job.

George milled through the crowd and noticed Abs was there with about four friends, talking to a few girls. As George approached Abs, he glanced and gave a nod to engage his attention. It worked and Abs acknowledged him with a little thumbs up.

George was suddenly joined by a few accomplices (two of Eddy's men, who had been sent up to sort this Abs episode out) who he didn't know. One whispered in his ear, "Keep walking and sit in that little corner bit." George was quietly escorted to the place by Eddy's man.

George was with a few friends and these newly found acquaintances; his mates wanted to go for a dance but George said he was preoccupied. His friends didn't know what he was going on about so went to the dance floor anyway.

The Irish boys saw Abs rise from his seat and ushered George up to follow him. Luckily, he was on his own and so there would be no collateral damage, George thought. George and the Irish boys followed Abs and, sure enough, he was heading to the toilets. The smoke emitted from the fog generator put a layer and haze around the club and it was hard to spot anyone in the smog. This was perfect. Abs got to the toilets, pushed the door firmly and entered.

About a minute later George and the Irish boys entered. One of them stayed at the entrance so no one could come in.

Abs was going to the toilet, oblivious to who was in there, and a couple of boys were looking in the mirror and doing their hair. George signalled for them to get out. They scooted away quite quickly, looking at the size of the Irish lad with George.

George took a step towards Abs and thought he'd better make sure it was him.

"Abs?" George said.

Abs looked round and answered, "Yes, who wants to know?"

"I'm sorry," George said and then fired the fatal shots, two towards the chest. Abs fell to the ground instantly with a scream.

George looked towards the Irish boy and they ran; the other one joined them and they raced uncontrollably towards the exit, knocking people flying, drinks flying and a lot of abuse was hurled at them by onlookers. There was absolute mayhem and hysterical cries from boys and girls in the club; some near to the toilets had heard the muffled gunshots, even though it had a silencer on, and were in a panic.

George and the Irish boy pushed through out of the club and a security guy on the Irish family payroll guided them out.

Up screeched two Range Rovers. One was for the Irish boys to return to HQ and brief Myles on events.

Before he knew it, George was in the back of the other Range Rover with his dad and his girlfriend.

An Irish guy was in front and shouted, "Seat belts on; we're off." The Range Rover screeched away into the night.

The family was driven to an airstrip for light aircraft just outside Guildford. Myles owned the land and did some business in and out of the country from that place. They were guided to a small aircraft.

"Here's a phone, an address, and we have transferred money into your account that will keep you going. It's destined for Scotland and a little town near Aberdeen."

"OK," Stephen said; he had been briefed on how events would go after the shooting.

"Don't come down south or to England and don't talk, as we can get to you."

Stephen, his girlfriend and George boarded the small aircraft for their new life.

CHAPTER 26

Myles was in the boardroom and Patrick was with him; they were discussing a few bits of business. As normal, Conor was sitting in the corner on his computer, his headphones on. Conor loved his computer and liked just being around the activity, even though he didn't participate. Occasionally he hacked into and bugged certain people's phones and did a bit of CCTV disablement, but that was it.

Myles broke away from his conversation with Patrick.

"Conor, what the fuck are you doing on that computer? You're always on it; don't you get sick of it? You're a fucking retard!" Myles shouted in Conor's direction.

Conor looked up. He was used to verbal abuse and bullying from a lot of the family – he would shrug it off.

"I'm p-p-playing a w-war game on the computer; it's good fun, Dad," Conor stammered back.

"OK, but take some time off it later. Go for a walk in the grounds with your sister or something. Yes, take the dogs for a run," Myles replied.

"OK, Dad," Conor said quietly and nervously.

"Get some fresh air and exercise," Patrick added, to reinforce

Myles' concern.

Myles didn't recognise Conor as integral to the family, just on the periphery, and they left him to his own devices, literally. Seamus and Eileen were his favourites, even though they should all have got his unconditional love and protection.

Myles turned to Patrick and continued.

"This off-duty or undercover policeman from the club, do you know his whereabouts?" Myles said.

"Yes, we have a few places and times; he does a running circuit. He's regular as clockwork: he does a country bike ride or a run most evenings down some lanes where he lives. Is it time now?" Patrick enquired.

Myles looked into Patrick's eyes with venom, as if to say *That's a dumb question.*

"Yes, sort it tonight; we can't wait another day," Myles exclaimed. "I want him dead and I don't want his body found." Myles got up and walked towards the door to exit the room. On the way he pushed Conor's laptop on to the floor in frustration and was very annoyed with Patrick's complacency about this cop.

Conor scrambled on the floor, picking the device up and checking it was all right. He was furious with his dad.

LATER THAT DAY – LATE AFTERNOON

Patrick assembled a few men from the house and picked up a couple from a local travelling community *en route* to the policeman's neighbourhood. Myles and Patrick used these guys for hits and disposing of evidence, in particular dead bodies. It was in Rickmansworth, not far, and Patrick knew the area quite well from some protection rackets they had going on with some pubs.

It would take about half an hour. There were four of them; they had balaclavas, night-vision goggles and some revolvers with silencers on. Patrick had worked out from his previous surveillance on the policeman where and how during the run he would do it.

"Love, I'm just going out for my run," Dave called up as he shut the front door.

"It's a bit dark out there – be careful," his wife returned.

"OK. I am a policeman, I can look after myself, love," he quipped back. He had a stopwatch function on his digital watch. He always wanted to beat his previous best; it was his competitive nature, and probably why he was in the police force. He liked the training they would do, including running, basic exercise, push-ups, press-ups, star jumps etc.

He got down to the end of the path then turned right. Normally his circuit was about three to four miles depending on how enthusiastic he was feeling. Dave started with a light jog, picked up the pace gradually for the next 200 yards, then reached his peak speed. It had just started to rain ever so slightly and the trees were swaying gently, indicating a small breeze that evening.

Meanwhile, Patrick and his small gang had reached the circuit they knew David had taken, and two men jumped out the back of a blacked-out van with tinted windows all round. Dressed in camouflage and khaki trousers, they lay in wait for the policeman to pass the intended point where they would gun him down. Dusk was just falling; Patrick was in the van with one of the travellers from the gypsy site near the McGinley's dwelling.

"You know we have to move swiftly. Get the body in the van, wrapped and put in a body bag. It's all in the back – you know what to do," Patrick ordered the accomplice. The boy was only eighteen or so but had been involved in a few hits already, including making bodies disappear. He was a second cousin to Myles and was trusted; he came up to the stately home (HQ) every other day for English lessons – just pronunciation and elocution – and some firing practice with various guns. Added to this Judith and Eileen would advise on dress codes to avoid looking like so-called travellers.

Dave was about a mile and a half into his jog and was entering a cut-through that passed an abandoned building, just near the end of a local industrial estate. Unbeknown to him, the Irish boys lay in wait in the derelict building. The entrance had no door, the building had graffiti on it and some old sleeping bags; it had obviously been used by some homeless individual recently. The Irish lads held their breath as there was a combined odour of urine and beer emanating from the building.

Out jumped one of the lads, revolver in hand. Dave approached but had no time to react, even with his police training. He was about three or four yards from his assailant.

POP-POP. A double entry to Dave's body. He hit the ground instantly, and he started to wriggle but he could not get away. The other accomplice walked over and finished with one shot to the head. A minute later the van pulled up and the side sliding door was opened. The three men picked up and bundled the police officer's body into the back and the van took off in a flash.

The gang drove to a local lake that was in the depths of a forest. The van was parked and they took the body in the bag and walked the fifty yards. Once at the edge of the water they walked in – they had fishermen's boots on. It was getting deep and there was a slight current. They threw the body as far as they could, then shuffled out of the water fast. The boys who had done the shooting launched both guns into the lake as well.

Back in the van they confirmed the deed was done. Patrick started up the engine and pulled away.

CHAPTER 27

BBC NEWS

"More news today: the fatal killing of a young boy in London last week has been linked to gang warfare between rival ethnic groups. A spokesman for the mayor of London said this is now 115 killings this year and intends to address this as an ongoing growing concern. The boy was believed to be aged seventeen and a promising football star.

"Lastly some good news: an old-age pensioner war veteran proposed to his long-term girlfriend of seventy-three years. When asked why it had taken so long, he jested, saying he did not want to rush into anything. He is aged ninety-seven."

Myles grinned about both bits of news. It seemed the hit on the boy wouldn't even flag back to them, so that was great. He had literally got away with murder.

Myles' family was holding meetings with different families on speakerphone/conference calls. It was growing apparent that the new gangs to fear and watch out for were eastern European, and Albanians in particular.

"Jack, you need to keep an eye on this as this is mainly on your patch, south of the river. They're making too much noise

– they will need to be taken down a peg or two. In fact, arrange a meet in the next two weeks. I want to talk face to face and get a translator," Myles said.

Jack was up at the manor today as he was on some reconnaissance for an imminent job regarding a shipment of drugs coming in on a chartered plane, believed to be from Norfolk way. Jack had run it past Myles, and it was just to seize the goods and knock over the pilot and anyone on the flight. There was a little airstrip near Norfolk but they didn't know on what day it was going to happen.

Eileen came into the room and beckoned her dad over for a chat. Myles went over to the window, away from everyone; obviously Eileen did not want her conversation being heard by anyone.

"Dad, I understand you have the boy; can you just rough him up a bit and let him go? Oh, and I've seen a dress I like – will you come up west with me today and buy it for me?" Eileen pleaded on both requests.

"The dress – fine, go with your mum and get it. She's got a joint credit card; treat yourselves to a meal in John Lewis, I know you both like it in there. As for the boy – no; he's messed with the wrong girl and the wrong family. I am dealing with that in the next few days," Myles said firmly.

Eileen was exasperated that he couldn't even come out with her for a few hours – business always took priority. As for this boy, she had never wanted this to happen. It was just a yarn to grab her father's attention. Never, never did she want an innocent person to die because of her lies.

Myles started to walk back to the boys and wrap up the meeting.

"Great, you can't even spare an hour or so with me! Work, work, work!" Eileen screamed as she stormed off.

The room fell silent for a few minutes, then Seamus cracked a joke to lighten the mood and get the meeting back on track.

"That rant was on a three – you should see her on her time of the month!" Seamus joked and grimaced at the same time.

The group descended into laughter and they picked up where they'd left off. Conor was in the corner of the room, on his computer as usual. and they left him to it.

Myles looked round the table and drew everybody's attention to the last problem on the agenda.

"This boy, Nick. I can't have him around anymore for two reasons – what he did and put Eileen through and the hurt brought on Judith and me, plus he's been to our hideaway. In hindsight, not a great move, but I wanted to talk to him, make him sweat a week or two. Make him think about his actions. There's a good chance he could recollect some incriminating info and we know he has already been to the police. I want this laid to bed now.

He is holed up at a relative's up north. I have arranged for local support from the Murphy family to get him down ASAP, possibly later today or tomorrow at the very latest," Myles said, concluding the meeting.

Everyone in the meeting went their separate ways apart from Myles, Patrick and Seamus; they remained in the room and spoke about matters that did not concern outside-family members. Conor stayed as normal playing computer games and having the odd Jack Daniel's and Coke. Conor was not a big drinker like Myles, Patrick and Seamus.

"Seamus, remember what I said – when I get this Nick down, I want you to pull the trigger. Do it for your sister and me," Myles said, looking deep into Seamus' eyes.

"OK, Dad." Seamus was shaking a bit but his dad did not notice.

The following day Myles contacted his local firm near where Nick was holed up; some gang runners had confirmed he was still at his aunt's.

"OK, go today, do the gas-board trick," Myles instructed.

"Yes, boss," said the gang member.

Later that day the gang gained access to the aunt's by posing as British Gas maintenance people on the pretence that they were checking the boiler. Once in, they went upstairs and knocked Nick unconscious and brought him down. Nick's aunt tried to stop them but got a firm smack across the face, knocking her to the floor. Nick was in a van and on the way back to the local Irish dwelling within twenty minutes.

Nick finally came round and he was in a helicopter with two other men and a pilot. He was awake for the final half an hour of the trip. It appeared they had used the M1 as their guide down south, and moments later it was landing in the grounds of a stately house. It was the same house he had been taken to about a week ago, where the nightmare had begun and now, he worried, where it would end.

CHAPTER 28

Finally, they knew the location, thanks to the GPS bug embedded on Nick Scott, and a location was beamed out. *Technology is brilliant*, Dantry thought. It was a mansion just on the outskirts of Guildford called "The Furlings". The building was about 300 years old, set in twenty acres of land. Information on the building and grounds was that it had been purchased about twenty years ago, but not in the name of McGinley. The Land Registry and deed details were in another name: Mr Lawrence. On further digging, it appeared there was no Mr Lawrence, no details could be found. It was a Grade II listed building and thus no change could be made without proper plans being submitted then approved.

Dantry was worried that the bug would be found on Nick by Myles or the gang members, so with this in mind a decision was made to do the raid ASAP, the next day. This was not ideal but a lot of plans were needed for this type of mission. If Myles found the bug, god only knew what the consequences would be. Nick would be executed immediately, for sure, but added to that Myles would know the police were on to him and wind the operation up and move out overnight.

It is all coming to a head, Dantry thought; he couldn't come this far and fail at the final hurdle. So many man hours had been put in, and a police officer killed in connection to Myles' exploits. Still only a suspicion but he was convinced evidence would confirm it and he was determined to get justice for the young policeman's widow and family.

Early looks from satellite imagery of the property indicated the layout had been changed and outbuildings added. One looked like a rifle shooting building. Some stables had been added with some horses picked up on satellite photos.

Dantry knew from the interview and phone calls from Nick that they could plan to execute him at any time. So, with this in mind he had to work with relevant army police, crack teams, to devise a plan to bust Nick out and arrest the Myles and Patrick roadshow. It was paramount they moved quickly with good backup. As Myles was ex-IRA, they could have a heavy arsenal of weapons and serious firepower.

The detail of these plans were with an elite crack team within the police and they would work on it ASAP, getting the relevant vehicles, firepower and specialist personnel who did these raids. Typically, they would be trained at army level, even SAS-trained at times. Heavy artillery would be required, and top-level radio equipment to report back to a commanding tactical officer. Dantry would be in a vehicle near the house with the tactical officer. Pictures and photos were circulated to all the men on the mission, so they knew the family members: Myles, Patrick, Seamus, Eileen, Conor and Judith. Obviously, they had an up-to-date picture of Nick and also prominent figures in Myles' gang, like Jack.

It was decided and, as often was the case, the raid would happen very early in the morning, maybe 4 a.m. It would be a dual attack on land and by police helicopters. About thirty to forty men would be despatched. Some real-time imagery would be relayed back from night-vision goggles/cameras they would be wearing.

Dantry's ultimate goal was Nick's safety, but bringing down the McGinley empire followed a close second. He had been told everything was in place and awaited his instructions. Ideally, he would like to get a message to Nick but this would not be possible.

CHAPTER 29

After meticulous planning, the raid was on. It really was not known what firepower they would be coming up against. They had got plans of the house and satellite images of the property and grounds, but it would still be difficult to know what they might encounter. It was established that the property was over three floors, and there were secret rooms above and underground.

In the last twenty-four to thirty hours there had been painstaking research and hard detailed surveillance; they would have liked more time but they were not afforded that luxury. Dantry's team had being working long shifts so they were as prepared as they could be. He did not want an innocent member of the public and a key witness dying – he would feel so guilty. He had a duty to save this Nick and felt for him being pulled into this awful episode. It was all about decision-making and he hoped this one was right.

The satellite images they had of the house and grounds showed that there were four static caravans to the rear of the house. It was not known what the headcount was in there and in the house; Dantry anticipated in excess of fifty, possibly.

The place had CCTV all the way down the drive and in the house, possibly in some of the static caravans, probably in all the rooms as well.

The GPS signal had Nick located in a small room on the top floor. A couple of men were stationed outside the door, and on the same level were other rooms probably housing more foot soldiers. The plans of the house and thermal imaging revealed Myles was on the first floor next to his office and Patrick had a separate room on the same level. On the ground floor it appeared five or six men were patrolling in and out of the grounds, doing shifts, so that meant twenty-four-hour coverage. Also on the ground floor was the room for Eileen and a guest room that Judith retreated to on those nights Myles was out with the lads, coming in late, or not at all.

The McGinleys, and Myles in particular, would not know of this imminent raid; he would have had no suspicions. Nothing to flag up that anything was leaked, wrong or that they were being monitored. A bit of noise surrounding Seamus' activities, but apart from that, nothing major to worry about.

The sun was just rising, the birds were cackling in their own language, and along the dirt track four blacked-out Range Rovers travelled, throwing up dust and dirt as they sped along the drive up to the house. Simultaneously, two helicopters glided along 100 feet off the ground, just above the nearby tree canopy line. They had instructions to land at the back and come in through the kitchen. There was a small landing area they could use fifty yards away from the static caravans. It would be a dual attack into the mansion causing maximum confusion and mayhem, Dantry hoped.

The helicopters landed and five men jumped out of each. They had black clothing on, night-vision goggles, plus hand-held machine guns; these were military personnel that police drew upon for these types of raids and missions. Everyone had been detailed on who was who, all had studied photos of the family gang members and known associates that might be there.

At the precise same time, at the front of the house, the Range Rovers pulled up outside poised.

All officers were on walkie-talkie contact and airwaves to the tactical officer. He was near to the house with Dantry, looking at images they could get from satellite, and reacting to events where possible. Some officers had body cams on. It was all high-tech surveillance and camera equipment relaying real-time feedback of all movements. It was basically a military manoeuvre.

A few seconds later, the whole household awoke to gunfire and people entering the building. Myles ran to all the rooms, screaming to everyone to get tooled up, which meant firearms. Shots were being fired by the police as well as flares and tear gas as they advanced deeper into the building on their mission.

"It's a siege, a hit or something! Everybody to their designated places!" Myles screamed out.

Eileen ran into Judith's room and they bolted the door, huddled in the corner. Conor remained in his room, which was on the second floor; no one, including Myles, expected him to participate in the defence of the house. As far as Myles knew, Conor didn't know one end of a gun from the other.

In meetings, the McGinleys would occasionally play out the

scenario of what would need to be done if a hit or a police raid happened. Myles made sure there was plenty of ammunition to hand in cabinets in most rooms. Rifles, machine guns and machetes were strategically placed around the house, and Myles and Patrick had them in their rooms.

The Irish gang members returned fire within seconds and bullets rained down on the vehicles at the front of the mansion. One of the officers went down, and blood was spurting out from his chest area. The police returned fire at the front door and up at the windows on the first floor. At the same time, the army personnel attached to the police broke in through the back door and despatched anyone who came their way. They were detailed to search and destroy, and if possible, capture Myles, Patrick and Seamus and to get Nick out alive.

The armed police broke down the front door and shot a few people they met in the large foyer. They proceeded along the ground floor and met with half-dressed Irishmen screaming and randomly shooting. All of those were put down by officer shots, about six to eight. Some officers received fatal shots from the Irish foot soldiers. It was a bloody gun battle.

Some of the lead force reached Judith's room, and it was locked. They broke it down and burst in.

They looked in and confirmed it was two women and assumed there would be no imminent trouble from them, but they were of the McGinley clan; built-in survival and fighting instincts ran through their veins.

"Stay here!" the officer said to the women.

A shot was fired from one of the women, later to be confirmed as Eileen. It hit the officer in the shoulder and he dropped to the floor. Another officer shot back at Eileen, wounding her in the leg with two shots. Once Eileen was down, he went over and cuffed her and her mum on some bed railings, then left the room quickly.

The gas canisters thrown into the house earlier were now making it very foggy throughout. The gypsies and foot soldiers from the caravans had come in the back to counter-attack the assault from the police; there were about ten of them and they were armed with sawn-off shot guns and pistols and Uzi machine guns.

There was utter mayhem all over the household and the shoot-out went on for about five or ten minutes. To everyone involved it probably seemed like hours.

The outcome was thus – Myles was captured and Patrick was killed on the stairs. Nick was found in the room they expected to find him in. He was handcuffed to a cabinet and the guards were gone. A lot of Irishmen fled once Patrick was killed and many arrests were made. Judith and Eileen were arrested and taken into custody for questioning about this night and the family's criminal involvement, which included a known policeman's murder and numerous other offences. Later, documents with Myles' signature were found that would be used subsequently in the trial, bribery and attempted murder amongst the offences.

Conor was found in his room playing on a computer, and an officer was found dead in the room. It was not proved or thought it was anything to do with Conor. On finding Conor, the police officers confirmed he was mentally unstable and had the mental age of a child. Seamus was not on the premises and was later picked up as he approached the property by police in an unmarked vehicle.

Nick was taken down to the station to give a statement of what had happened and all the information he had heard whilst held captive. He was mentally exhausted, but the police insisted it had to be collated and documented whilst fresh in his mind.

The stats for the shoot-out numbered six policemen killed and twenty-two Irish family members killed, including Patrick McGinley.

The stately home was evacuated, and about twenty Irish men and women from caravans were taken into custody for questioning, to try to see where they fitted in the larger picture of the crime syndicate. Some had fled into the surrounding fields but most were captured. Police forensic teams were sent to the scene that night and the property and road sealed off to anyone apart from police.

Dantry was pleased on the whole about the operation, but devastated that six colleagues had perished and that he would have to have the horrible conversations with the widows and family. Now came the hard work of putting the case, allegations and accusations together which would take weeks before there was any hope of going to trial.

CHAPTER 30

Nick had received a superficial wound in the melee of the police crack team trying to get him out alive. It had happened so quickly he was not sure if it had been from the Irish mob or a stray bullet from the armed police. The previous night, before the police raid, he'd had a bit of a kicking from Myles and Seamus. He had bruising around the side of the head, had lost a tooth and still had a banging headache. In his statement he told Detective Dantry how Myles had said he was due to be executed the next day (which turned out to be the raid day) and Seamus was to be his executioner. So the raid had been done just in time before the execution.

The stately house, known as The Furlings, had come under a brutal attack from the military-style raid from the police. Rooms, buildings and grounds had been decimated in the ordeal; parts looked like footage you would see in reels from the Second World War on the PATHÉ news. Forensic teams were still on-site gathering evidence, DNA, looking through CCTV and personal computer systems. It would take a lot of time to unravel what had happened on the shoot-out, plus looking at the day-to-day running of the firm.

Whilst going through the CCTV footage they saw the whole episode of how Patrick, number two of the gang, had died. As the raid was going on it became apparent the police had the upper hand, so footage from a few different rooms showed how Patrick ushered and led Myles away to an upstairs room. As this played out, the leaders of the armed response team tracked them, putting down any loyal followers they came across. It was probably three to four minutes into the mission that they finally confronted Patrick and Myles; it appeared from the footage that they asked them to surrender.

Moments later, Patrick went to fire off shots and that was when one of the police officers made the decision to take the fatal shot at Patrick. Myles then fell to the floor and tried to revive Patrick, but in the end, he knew he was dead. In a rage, Myles rose to his feet and pulled a gun from his coat; the officer told him to put it down and to think of his wife and children. Myles hesitated but realised there were a few guns on him; he could see the red dots. He reluctantly dropped the firearm and fell to his knees, surrendering. The officers moved in and arrested him.

Another camera showed the footage of Eileen pulling the trigger and firing at an officer. She would later plead in court that this was in self-defence. The CCTV camera where Conor was had been disabled and no video footage was found. Conor had been found in the corner of his room playing on his computer, and a dead policeman was also in there – one shot to the middle of the forehead.

On being interviewed he said the policeman stumbled

into the room and fell to the ground, then died from his wounds. The investigating team's detective sergeants believed this story, as all the family said Conor was not involved with criminal activity; in fact, he loathed it. The interviewing officer confirmed he had some mental health issues and could not believe he could have killed someone; therefore, he believed the sequence of events Conor had described. It was noted he was very nervous and stuttered heavily during questioning.

Dantry and his team would now have to put a case together for Myles and the players of the organisation, notably Seamus, Jack and Eileen. Most importantly for Dantry, was getting some of the witnesses and people who would give evidence against Myles and the family into safe houses. A couple of distant relatives of Myles had given evidence/ratted against him to get shorter sentences and this was a definite no-no within the criminal fraternity – they would be high risk, thus would be put into safe dwellings until the trial.

Nick was the one most at risk because of the rape allegation and his being in the house on two separate occasions. Myles would see this as his priority hit. With this in mind, Dantry sorted Nick's safety first – and quickly. They did not want to have him too far away as there were still statements and details to go through.

It was decided Leicester was far enough away, but near enough to go and get statements and check on him. It was explained to Nick he would go straight to the safe house until further notice. The most dangerous period and time to seek revenge were the days and weeks after the trial. Myles' gang would still be running fairly smoothly, even though who would be running things would be unknown.

Myles and the rest of the family were under arrest and in police custody, in an undisclosed police building. Dantry and Scrivener were aware that someone from the organisation might try to break Myles out of jail. Based on this assumption he was under twenty-four-hour surveillance at a fortress-like location.

On the whole Dantry was pleased with the raid and the people they had taken down – it was just a case now of getting justice and long sentences for them all.

CHAPTER 31

Detective Dantry, Detective Scrivener, Constable Cook and the team now had the task to piece together a case against Myles, Patrick and his cronies. The bug fitted to Nick had given Dantry precise coordinates of his location and house he was held captive in. All the time during the investigation they could never trace Myles or family members to the address. On numerous occasions he had been tailed but Myles' people had a knack of knowing and would shake them off.

Dantry was relieved that Myles had not instructed a body search as that could have ended in instant death for Nick. Myles was arrogant; it came to light he thought he was of interest to the police, but oblivious to how close they were to the organisation. He knew Seamus had cocked up but hadn't done anything incriminating. The evening at the gents' club he thought was nothing too serious, but this did aid the investigation – and the evidence from the police officer was crucial to the case. Slowly but surely Dantry was putting a dossier together of his criminal activities.

Whilst looking through jobs and hits, a name kept recurring; just his first name – Cyril, no reference to a surname. It seemed a common theme that when a hit was required, more often than not, he was summoned. He seemed like a ghost; there were no photos of him, no address, no phone number. There were no unaccounted people in photos of the family and associates except for this Cyril. In the hit on the Scouse gang drug deal, he was mentioned to have been involved and gunned down four or five people. His name also came up on other hits, as far away as Brazil in one case.

After two weeks' constant work by Dantry, Scrivener and the investigating team, a case was submitted with supporting evidence to the Crown Prosecution Service. Dantry was pleased with all their efforts and thought there would be no way they would get off scot-free. In his mind the prosecution would put a damning case forward and convince the jury of Myles' and his family's guilt. Myles and his gang were going down for many years.

On closer inspection, nothing was linked to Judith or Conor so no charges were brought against them. Dantry suspected Judith must have been involved but nothing was found in documents, notes or diaries that were kept at the house. A safe was found in an attic, containing false ID, money in different currencies, passports in different names, etc. The police had recovered about £200,000 in unused notes, and substantial amounts of heroin and cocaine as well.

Dantry checked every day with key witnesses who were in safe houses and they all fully intended to give evidence. No one was having any second thoughts and they all remained brave enough to testify against Myles and the family.

He did come back to thinking about Conor; he seemed a mystery, an enigma in it all. Did he kill the police officer found in the same room as him? *Surely, he must have some role in the family's activities*, Dantry thought, but there was no evidence anywhere to support his hunch.

It was just a matter of time before the trial date came round. He looked forward to finishing up on this and moving on. Dantry was not far off retirement and said to himself he would just do two more years. He had promised his wife they would retire out to Tuscany. He pondered on his career, and though on the whole, it had been a success, a few unsolved cases had beaten him. This one was his biggest and most satisfying, although it would not put much of a dent in the criminal trades out in the UK. He thought it was extremely rewarding to take this murderer and gangster along with his top associates off the streets for a very long time.

CHAPTER 32

Eileen, Judith, Conor and other members of the family and close associates had to flee the family home in Guildford. Eileen was on bail pending the court case against her. The family home had been shot to pieces on the stake-out. Rooms had been literally blown apart, hanging walls, ceilings and doors all in ruins. It was now a major crime scene with policemen and forensic scientists combing it like archaeologists trying to find some lost artefacts.

Due to the severity of the allegations against Myles, Seamus, Jack and a few others, they were in police custody with no bail granted, heavily guarded in an unknown police location. It was a safe house as it was feared Myles' people would try and get him out somehow. Eileen and Judith were to have some allegations against them but weren't considered a threat to the general public so, released on bail, they had to report to their local police station every day; they were under strict curfew. Conor, as far as the police knew, was not involved in any criminal activity so was not under any such curfew. When questioned, the interviewing officer said he could hardly string a sentence together and kept asking when he could go and play on his computer.

The police were uncovering a lot of information on jobs and hits etc. Whilst at the house Dantry noticed many rooms remained but worked out they had different functions. One room looked like a solicitor's office with many law books on the shelves, another room for finance, another linguistics. It was a sophisticated operation that he could not have imagined.

"I can't believe the level of detail there is in this house and the modifications that have been done," Dantry said to Scrivener.

"How long do you think they have been operating, boss?" Scrivener replied.

"I don't know – ten or fifteen years? We know Myles and Patrick were prevalent in the IRA and it is believed they were doing their own scores away from the leaders of the IRA – just racketeering, intimidation etc.," Dantry said. Late 1990s the intensity was stepped up by the McGinley family once the ceasefire as such was declared.

Another police officer came into the room.

Dantry gave him a long stare. "Have you found any information about bank accounts, offshore accounts or deposit accounts?" Dantry asked, frustrated, fully expecting the answer still to be no.

"I'm afraid not, sir; no deposit transactions, no transfers, no bank statements, nothing. A grand-scale operation like this would have deposit accounts and offshore accounts like you say, but nothing has been uncovered in that area," the sergeant said.

"Keep looking; they will turn up I'm sure," Dantry said. "Maybe I will grill Myles to find out some info when I see him tomorrow in custody," he continued.

Detective Scrivener joined the discussion. "Guv, there's loads of CCTV footage from all the rooms; video files on their server. This is taking many man hours to go through. We imagine there will be a lot of incriminating evidence. Especially on the night of the raid!" Scrivener said positively.

"Good work. OK, we will reconvene tomorrow at nine o'clock sharp and put case files together against them individually for all the offences," Dantry concluded.

Meanwhile, at a cousin's house, Eileen and Judith were in a meeting considering their options on how to plead to their charges. They had their attorney present, advising. It was apparent that evidence would incriminate them in involvement but a long sentence was unlikely. However, the attorney said Eileen would be in trouble for shooting a policeman.

Eileen was worried about this. Her attorney was advising her to own up before footage could be found on CCTV. She was extremely stressed out.

Conor came to the door and waved Eileen to come over. She wondered what he might want, so got up and followed him down the hall to another room. They went in and Conor shut the door and they sat down.

"Conor, what do you want? I've got some serious shit I need to talk about with Mum and the solicitor. You're all right – there are no allegations against you!" she exclaimed, exasperated.

"I'm too clever to get caught," Conor said.

Eileen smirked and then said, "You're a dimwit, just like Dad says."

She went to leave and Conor got up, blocked her way and pushed her down firmly. As far as Eileen knew, Conor could not have any relevant info to talk about, and that's if he could even spit it out anyway. She was frustrated and wanted to get to the matters in hand.

"Eileen, I could get you off, but I won't. I don't like you. I don't believe this story you made up about this Nick. I've done some digging around on this – it's not sat well with me," Conor said firmly.

"You can't get me off, you dimwit; I don't know how you've suddenly found your tongue. The rape happened," she said, confused. Eileen wondered how and why Conor was suddenly talking. All these years he'd kept himself to himself and pretended he couldn't talk. Had he been acting all this time?

This was not very important to her now – her main concern was seeing how she could get off with a lighter sentence. That was why she was talking to her mum, to see if anything could be done.

Once again, she motioned to get up and Conor shoved her down into the back of the settee. "The rape. Did it happen? I don't recall you going to Herts the time and day you say it happened," Conor probed.

"Yes, it happened; what's it to you anyway?" she shouted, getting up for a third time. She brushed past Conor and made her way back to the room to continue discussions with Judith and the family attorney.

"You're my sister, I have to look out for you!" Conor replied.

"Yeah, right; I have to look after you more like!" she shouted as she walked down the hallway back to her mum.

"They won't find anything on Mum, I've seen to that," Conor shouted as Eileen walked away.

Eileen dismissed the comment; she knew there would be documents that would lead back to her mum. They were all going down, she thought.

CHAPTER 33

After four weeks and one of the longest trials for this type of case in UK history, a verdict was given. In the process, there were countless witnesses in the court, on video-link, cross-examination, defence lawyers and prosecution lawyers, statements from police and statements from the Irish family members indicting Myles, Patrick (even though he was dead), Seamus and Eileen.

Added to this there were other members of the syndicate in other areas of the country involved in all the offences. There were hundreds of documents, pictures, written statements, audio recordings and much CCTV video footage. This evidence had been heard by twelve members of the jury, the presiding judge and the media – well, the few allowed in. TV cameras were in the court every day. This trial had stirred up a lot of media attention.

Some of the McGinley associates had turned on Myles and provided incriminating information, and in return they were offered a deal and a lesser sentence. In particular was the family up north, who'd arranged to get Nick back down to Myles' place. Dantry had really squeezed them to get confessions and information. His team had worked painstakingly long hours going over and over evidence for the Crown Prosecution Service.

The shoot-out had been crucial in bringing a grander case against Myles and the family, they being found guilty of killing police officers when they had been asked to lay down their weapons on a few occasions during the siege.

Myles was caught on his own CCTV firing a fatal bullet to the temple of an officer who was clearly down and wounded and could not defend himself. It even showed the wounded officer put his arms up as if to say *Don't shoot*.

CCTV footage and recordings also had Myles the night before saying that Nick would be executed the next day on account of the rape. Other evidence also included audio dialogue from the gents' club and a notebook relating to the hit on the off-duty policeman.

Seamus was charged with murder, kidnap, intimidation and serious assault on two individuals. Information had been gathered by an associate turning against him. It was inferred the family had killed the undercover policeman who went to the gents' club the night Seamus had the altercation with the Asian lad. For this particular offence they only had circumstantial evidence, like blood stains in a vehicle that matched the police officer's blood type. As the body had not been found, it could not be proved they had killed him. He was technically injured and missing until a body was found.

Eileen was found guilty of attempted murder on a policeman. The policeman's statement read that he had asked the two women to stay put and to lock the door. When his back was turned Eileen had opened fire on him, causing significant injury. It was expected it would take the officer nine to twelve months to rehabilitate.

Jack, the head of the London unit, was found guilty of conspiracy to murder the boy Abs. It did not come to light who killed Abs, but he had planned and orchestrated it. The name Cyril was spoken about but, to date, his true identity and whereabouts were unknown; he was a ghost. Although Patrick had died in the siege, his offences were also read out.

So that was the end. It was now just a few hours' wait for the jury to deliberate and go through each member of the family's charges and the allegations against them. At the beginning of the case, two members of the jury had been replaced, as it had come to light that Myles' people had got to them and some bribery allegations were revealed.

Conor had no charges made against him, nor did his mum, and no family members or associates ratted on either of them. He seemed untouchable. The police were surprised; they thought there would be something, however little, but nothing was found. In fact, Conor had been in the court in the public gallery, just as an interested party to see what fate his family would get for their rap sheet.

Judith had some small references to involvement but nothing that could be connected to criminal activity, and Dantry had found this very strange.

Nick stood in the public gallery, trying to keep out of any spotlight. He thought about the last six or seven weeks, from the day he was kidnapped, to the siege, and about being rescued without too much injury. He'd had some cuts and bruises from the night before the siege at the hands of Seamus and Myles. They had now gone and he'd had his tooth replaced. He had been advised by Detective Dantry that he would not be able to go back to a normal life after this trial, so he would be starting a new life, a new journey, without his family and friends.

"Myles McGinley, you are found guilty on all counts put before you. Murder, attempted murder, kidnap, robbery, supply of class A drugs, intimidation and protection rackets," the judge announced.

"I am sentencing you to two concurrent life sentences and fifteen years for attempted murder. You will not be eligible for parole," the judge concluded.

A silence came over the courtroom. Then Eileen and Seamus had their sentences given out and another twelve family members would be jailed for multiple offences similar to those of Myles: aiding and abetting, kidnapping, conspiracy to murder, grievous bodily harm and burglary, to mention just a few.

Myles was led away, cuffed, but on the way out he hurled threats in the direction of the detective, Nick and the judge, saying he wouldn't forget today and that they were dead men walking. He was quickly taken from court.

There had been a cheer from the gallery; a few widows of the killed police officers were in attendance, plus people from Dantry's team. The detectives looked at each other and some of the team members, pleased with the verdicts and the sentences handed out. It had been a good result. Dantry and Scrivener disregarded the threat to their lives; they always got this, even from juveniles who'd been put away for drugs or lesser offences than the McGinley crowd.

CHAPTER 34

After the trial, Nick was taken straight to a safe house and the location was not disclosed to anyone, only a few policemen on the case. Protocol in these circumstances was family and friends were not told – for the good of the witness and the safety of the family. As Nick was driven away to a new life, it dawned on him that his life was going to change forever. He had not seen his family, friends or work colleagues for approximately six weeks; he had been in police protection from after the raid on the McGinleys' mansion until the trial. This was not unusual in this type of trial, with gangland mobsters convicted on evidence he had provided.

Nick had managed to ring his mum on a handful of occasions, but he missed her and the family dearly and knew he was resigned to a lonely new life without his close ones. It was going to be hard, he knew that. He hadn't asked to be drawn into this; it was that crazed Eileen girl who (it all came out in the trial) was trying to get her dad's attention. He thought it was not fair and he'd cried often at the safe house. It was lonely with no one to talk to. The police had provided counsellors and specialists to try and get him through, but it was very tough.

They had briefed him on his new life and the dos and don'ts in a witness protection programme, *And most of it is don'ts*, he thought to himself.

None of his work colleagues knew about the catalogue of events. Bill had an inclination Nick was involved or had been drawn into a web of uncertainty and it was serious, but did not know to what extent. Wayne had been let in a little; he knew about the Irish gang and the kidnap, and that Nick had subsequently had to leave work with no notice and go into hiding. He didn't know that Nick had been taken back to the McGinleys' house; Nick had mentioned the first incident, but because of the trial, Wayne would not know anything about the second occasion.

He had been in a temporary dwelling whilst the new life was being put together – location, ID, relevant documents and a new job. The realisation was sinking in on the journey up north. The policeman had said it would be in Cumbria, a six-hour drive from his soon-to-be old life. Driving up, he had an unbelievable urge to say his last goodbyes. The specialists had said no, it was not a good idea, because the rest of the Irish gang could be staking out his known haunts, workplace and family home.

Nick was playing everything through his mind over and over again; it could not pan out like this. He had one last thing he had to do.

"Stop, stop the car!" Nick called out to the driver and passenger. They were close colleagues to Detective Dantry and Scrivener.

The policeman stopped the car. They were in an unmarked police vehicle, a top-of-the-range Mercedes with blacked-out and bullet-proof windows. At least that's what they said when they collected him from the safe house. Both policemen were armed and had bullet-proof vests on, ready for any eventuality.

"What is it? We have to move quickly," the police officer said firmly. They took Myles' threats on Nick's life very seriously, and all the time they were down south, he was in danger.

"I have to say goodbye to my family and friends, I have to, especially my mum."

"No, we are under strict orders to take you up today. I know your predicament and how you must feel, but we have to be clinical and cannot take any risks!" the passenger-side policeman said.

"Rubbish! You don't know how I feel; I am never going to give my mum another hug, play golf with my dad, go to the pub with my brother, have a laugh with people at work. I will have to build a life from scratch, and these important people in my life that I will never see again can never be replaced," Nick said with a tone of despair.

The policemen looked at each other and could feel the desperation and pain from Nick.

"OK, we will take a round-robin trip, only five minutes at each place. You don't tell anyone within the police force – and especially not Dantry or Scrivener. We are putting our jobs on the line," the policeman said. "Turn the car round and head back down south; any repercussions, I will take full responsibility." He was a sergeant and the senior of the two.

The driver looked over his shoulder, waited for a couple of cars to go past, then pulled out with an abrupt U-turn, causing a skid, and proceeded in the opposite direction at great speed.

"OK, I presume your mum's house first?" the sergeant said.

"Yes," Nick replied.

About forty-five minutes later, they were outside the house. Nick paused; he could see his mum tending the garden, pruning her roses. He got out of the car and walked up the drive.

"Mum," Nick said and ran over to her. She looked up and moved towards her son. They met and embraced; Nick felt like he wanted it to last forever but knew he had to say his goodbyes rapidly.

"Oh, Nicholas, I've been so worried about you. I've been informed of the gravity of events and the peril you are in. You know I love you dearly. I know you are to go to a secret location and there is no other option," his mum said.

"I love you too. I have to go. I will see you again one day, I promise," he said, tears coming to his eyes. "Just want to say goodbye to Stephen and Dad; are they inside?" Nick said.

"Yes, I think they're in the lounge watching some football highlights," his mum said.

Nick looked round at the waiting police car and caught the gaze of the policeman who motioned at an imaginary or real watch to say, *We have to go.*

Nick came out of his house shortly after saying his emotional farewell to his family. He looked one last time at his mum and they both exchanged a glance to say they loved each other; no words needed. He jumped in the car and they set off towards

Wayne's place of work. It was only a few miles away.

As the police car approached the shop, they reiterated to Nick that he had to be quick. He understood and ran into the shop. It was quite busy; *Life and the world just carries on*, Nick thought. *What is life all about*? He parked that thought as it was a subject and a half.

He had to ask one of the shop assistants to call for Wayne. About a minute later, Nick saw him emerge from the back of the store, coming out of the stockroom. Nick saw him as an unofficial brother, and he was going to miss his friendship so much, but he knew he had to go.

As he approached Wayne, he was his normal-looking self, shuffling along with a broad grin, welcoming Nick.

"Wayne, so good to see you. How you keeping?" Nick said.

"Missed you, mate. I rang your house and your mum said you had to go away; is it because of what happened with that Irish crowd? Nutters!"

"Yes, mate, I can't explain. I'm going away for my safety. I had to testify in court about an incident," Nick said, choking up about his farewell. Wayne sometimes didn't realise the gravity of a conversation or an event. "You've been great to me – remember we've had some brilliant times. Give us a hug," Nick said.

Wayne looked a bit awkward but they embraced. Nick turned as he walked away. "I'll see you in the next life, mate; be good," Nick said, nearly in tears, it was so emotional. He got back into the car and said one last place: his work.

Nick asked them to pull in at the service yard at the back and the police agreed that would work well – fewer people to see them. He got out of the car and rang the bell; it was quite late and they would be closing up soon.

The back door opened and it was Jo-Anne. She was in utter disbelief as he had abruptly left the company about two months ago. She had a soft spot for Nick as well and neither had done anything about it.

"Hi, Jo, I've got to be quick," Nick said as he brushed past her and went into the back office. "Who's in?" he asked.

"It's just me and Bill; Daphne rang in sick. It's been a right struggle – you come to help out?" she said.

"Dressed like this, er, no, I don't think so. Get Bill and tell him to shut up shop for five minutes, put the sign on the front," Nick said, firmly drifting into manager mode.

Once all together, Nick explained he was OK, but he had to go away for a while as he had been embroiled in and was witness to some criminal dealings. "Come on, group hug, one last time," Nick said.

They had a hug. Nick was happy he had made his goodbyes, and who knew, one day he might see them again, he hoped. Jo-Anne was so upset she began to cry; Bill was fighting back the tears and Nick felt the same.

"OK, be good, you guys, and keep selling those insurances! Ker-ching!" Nick said, then went straight towards the back and out the door, feeling emotional. He turned and looked at Jo-Anne, and thought they could have been an item, but now he would never know if it would have worked out. Jo-Anne looked at Nick as he stepped into the car and had similar thoughts to his. She would miss him.

Nick got into the police car and said, "One more place?"

"No, we've been too long as it is! We are under strict orders to get you to your new place by today; it's going to be late as it is anyway," the sergeant insisted.

With that they started their journey up north, arriving in Cumbria around 9 p.m. The policemen left and said they would go through things tomorrow. Nick opened the house with the keys they gave him, shut the door, and burst into tears.

CHAPTER 35

Myles sat in his cell in Belmarsh; it had now been five months since his sentence. He had some good creature comforts and knew they all saw him as the new "daddy" of the establishment. Guards and wardens would give little luxuries and privileges that slightly softened the blow of being condemned to life behind bars. He had his own cell, TV, top-of-the-range hi-fi system and a comfortable bed. His cell was twice the size of your typical cell for prisons. At dinnertime he would quite often get his favourite or requested meal.

On further reflection, he thought about the great times and scrapes he'd had with his lifetime friend, Patrick. Running errands for the movement and cause, which led to him gradually rising up the ranks. He'd started off running notes between houses, then collecting monies for the cause and, as he reached his late teens, blackmailing shopkeepers for money.

This was where he'd met Patrick. He already knew Patrick as they were cousins, but a family feud meant they didn't mix. It was alleged that Patrick's father had had an affair with Myles' father's then partner. Anyway, their friendship developed and they were quite often paired for jobs, and outside this they would sink a fair few pints of Guinness at various pubs along and around the Falls Road area of Belfast

Myles met Judith about that time and their romance started. He remembered falling strongly for Judith. It was not long before they got wed, and it was a huge traditional Irish wedding. As in many marriages, the natural progression was to have babies and he thought he was fortunate to have three beautiful children.

Myles started to look back at his life; he had a lot of time on his hands now. Seamus, the eldest, he always had a deep bond, being the first; Eileen was second and his first girl, so felt he had to protect her and they had a close, strong relationship. Finally, Conor was born, and looking back now, Myles never really made a connection with him like he had with his first two. Maybe the intensity and his new position in the IRA caused this and he didn't have the time.

On reflection he did feel guilty, and he'd also felt upset about Conor's disability and mental issues, so had thought it best to leave it to Judith to deal with. These issues came about or were diagnosed when Conor was about ten years old. Myles found it hard to deal with; he was a man's man and saw this as weakness.

Now look where they all were. The whole family shattered, never to be whole again. His cousin and best friend Patrick, dead. Why didn't he go legitimate earlier? There had been times and opportunities to do so, and then they would've all been together, happy and comfortably well off. If only he'd followed his instincts. He had, on some days, been on the verge of lifting the family out and going AWOL, but he was too heavily involved.

Myles snapped out of feeling sorry for himself and thought about what had been consuming him for the last six months: vengeance and retribution.

Top of his list of targets were Detective Dantry, the judge, and Nick Scott, the boy who raped his daughter. Lower down the list but just as important were the turncoat family members up north. He knew he would not get a good night's sleep until this was all taken care of. It was difficult now he was inside to get someone to carry out his orders and his hits. It would have to be Jack's son. Jack had been involved in taking care of the Abs character that had beaten up his cousin.

Yes, Jack's son, James, would have to exact revenge or organise it on behalf of Myles. Myles penned a letter to James, detailing and writing in code what he wanted done. He knew the judge was in Italy, so he gave James details of a man who could take care of it in that region; he was tied into the Sicilian mafia, but Myles had collaborated with him on some European business. In return, Myles had taken care of some hits for the Italian family in London.

A few days later Myles had a conversation with one of the senior wardens about getting a letter out of the building without it being intercepted by the top brass of the prison, who weren't on Myles' payroll. He gave him £200 to do it.

A couple of days later, James received the letter from Myles. He was still getting regular money from the McGinley family to continue certain jobs – collecting money from clubs and restaurants, amongst other menial tasks. So, he was on the payroll and, despite Myles being in prison, he did not want to cross paths or disobey orders. Myles had stated that once all the hits were carried out, an extra £100,000 would be deposited in a Swiss account that he would give him access to.

Later that day, James set about putting things in motion: research, reconnaissance, resources and selecting personnel for jobs. Myles had previously sounded James out on this, but now it was real.

James had the perfect person for the hit on the detective. He dialled a number on his phone as he walked up and down his office. "Cyril, got a job for you – it's for Myles," James said.

James proceeded to detail the job.

"Give me the target; full name, last known address, photo, if possible. I will send you an email address – put the details in there. I will reply with bank details. It will only be able to receive emails for forty-eight hours, then I will close it. Normal rate that Myles pays: ten thousand pounds," Cyril said, then hung up.

CHAPTER 36

Dantry was living an idyllic lifestyle in the Cotswolds with his family that consisted of his wife, Mary, and his two daughters, Diane and Janice. It had now been nearly six months since the trial and sentence of Myles and his family members for the atrocities they'd carried out. It had been a painstaking investigation that had led to hundreds of hours of work and sacrifice for the family and his sanity. It nearly cost him his marriage; his job and his drive to put Myles and his associates away had been like a mistress, an addiction in some sense.

Dantry still remembered the outburst and message from Myles as he was led away to start his sentence. It haunted him, but he had had similar threats on previous cases and trials. It was the convicted's last furore, the last line, their last moment of notoriety. Dantry and his colleagues would often laugh, "If I had ten pounds every time a guilty person was going to kill me, I could have retired years ago."

As Dantry had such a great quality of life now, he felt it was a reward for his sacrifices back then. He loved his family and the time they all spent together. He had his little Jack Russell and his fish tank at home. He was content.

It was a lovely summer's evening and Dantry and his wife were having a lazy stroll in the country. The birds were singing and the trees were whispering as they rustled against each other. He was on his favourite trek that they would take every evening. The path opened up to a little field they would walk through, only five minutes from their house. He loved the peace and tranquillity. They were all under aliases and he had a part-time job in the charity shop in the village. It was different but they were all getting used to it now.

"This is the life. Didn't I promise you luxury and good things?" he said to his wife, Mary.

"Yes, you did; I'd hoped they'd happen earlier," she laughed, also very content with their new lifestyle. As they came to the end of the path, they went into the open field. They walked hand in hand, looking lovingly at each other and oblivious to the surroundings; they were on autopilot.

Opposite the opening, two men were walking, coming towards Dantry and his wife. Dantry noticed them and thought it was unusual – they rarely bumped into or came across anyone on their peaceful trek. He thought no more of it. They continued walking.

Bleep, bleep. A text came to Dantry's phone, and he thought it must be one of his daughters as there were only a few people who had the number. He rummaged around his lightweight jacket and pulled it out. He read the message. *Charles, meet your fate. Myles.*

How the hell had Myles got this number? He looked across at his wife. The men were now only twenty yards away and the next events all happened in nanoseconds. Time stood still, it seemed to Dantry.

"Myles says hello," Cyril shouted across the field.

He grabbed his wife's hand and told her to run. It was too late – four bullets were fired over a three- to four-second period. Three went into Dantry from behind and one hit his wife's leg.

The two Irishmen ran off, jumped on some nearby motorbikes and were away within seconds. Meanwhile Dantry's wife lay there, bleeding and in utter shock, screaming for help.

Detective Dantry passed away a few minutes later in his wife's arms.

CHAPTER 37

The judge, in summarising the McGinleys' case, labelled and described Myles as one of the most ruthless individuals he had ever come across. Judge McGregor, of Irish ancestry, said the deeds done and the cold-hearted murders were unimaginable and set an awful precedent to Myles family members and close associates. He went on to say that the family members were too scared to question decisions as they feared internal retribution.

It was one of the judge's last cases and he took early retirement shortly after it. The police authorities suggested it would be prudent. He was offered anonymity but quipped if he had taken that every time a convicted criminal was sentenced, he would have about ten aliases and countless residences all over the world.

Instead, he and his wife, Julie, decided to move to Italy and sample fine wines from the most famous vineyards in the Tuscany region. Judge McGregor was approaching seventy now and looked forward to a pleasant retirement with his wife, who was ten years his junior. They had a nice little nest egg, and the pension was a good sizeable amount each month.

It was now six months since the case. He had been highly

commended as he'd handed out maximum sentences to all the convicted members at the end of the trial. He now had a nice villa just outside Pisa, which was quaint, idyllic and they had great weather most of the year round. His wife enjoyed the garden and they had a small vineyard of their own that the judge tended, growing grapes that could be harvested for wine-making.

During one week in June, McGregor surprised his wife, saying that he would take her out for the day and they would visit the Leaning Tower of Pisa. She was looking forward to seeing the famous building.

They set off about 10 a.m. Once out of their villa, they proceeded on a single-track road that would get them the best part of the way towards Pisa. Despite it being single lane, it was a fairly busy thoroughfare as it was one of just a few roads that went to Pisa from the south.

Myles knew the judge was in Italy and was aware of his location, and from prison he had ordered the contract on the judge's head. James was organising it and, as it was in Italy, it went out to a few known outfits, with many notorious gangs keen to get the rewards. Myles and James had agreed that an Italian mafia gang would carry out the hit; it would make sense because they would blend in, they knew the area, spoke the language and were geared up for this type of hit.

A couple of miles into the journey, the judge's car started being tailed by a red Alfa Romeo. The trip to the tower was about ten miles so they were there after about twenty minutes. He parked at a paid car-park zone near the tower.

The judge got out of his car and ventured over to the ticket machine. The Alfa Romeo, carrying two people, pulled into the car park a few minutes afterwards; the occupants saw the judge get his ticket and parked twenty yards away from the judge's car.

The first Italian got out of his car and walked to the ticket machine, brushing past the judge, half knocking him off his feet and apologising unreservedly. The judge accepted the apology, went to his car and started the walk to the Pisa attraction with his wife. Julie was very excited as she was a keen enthusiast of history and historic buildings.

The Italian hitman quickly put the ticket in his car and, with his accomplice, started to follow the judge and his wife towards the tower. As they got nearer, the crowds started to get thicker and the pace slowed as people started to descend on a queue that was forming. Both the Italians tracked them but did not join the queue, they just continued to walk parallel to the line. This raised a few mumblings as people thought they intended to jump the queue; little did they know what was about to happen.

They both drew up alongside the judge and his wife, and one of the Italians leant into the judge and whispered, "Judge McGregor, Myles says hello and goodbye." At the same time as finishing the sentence, he plunged a long knife repeatedly into the judge.

The judge slumped into the Italian and he caught him and held him into his chest, then plunged the knife into his back for good measure. The judge was screaming, and people could not believe what was happening in front of them in broad daylight. The judge fell to the floor and blood started gushing out from all the wounds on to the sandy gravel track that led to the entrance to the tower. Julie bent over and cradled her husband. He managed to say goodbye, then passed away.

The Italians ran away to their car, and some onlookers were trying to find security or venue organisers to inform them what had just happened. By the time a policeman was found, the Italians were in their car and on the way back to their masters.

A couple of days later, word got back to Myles that the contract had been completed, and he in turn spoke to James and authorised the monies for the hit to be transferred to the Italian mafia gang who had carried it out.

CHAPTER 38

It was now six months since the trial. Nick had got to see the whole network of corruption and activity they were involved in when he was being prepared for his witness statement. His testimony about the kidnapping and the attempt on his life were key elements for the case and prosecution. Despite all the suspected criminal activity of Myles and the McGinley family, there were only three or four jobs that police had evidence and witness statements for. A lot of Myles' dirty work, including multiple murders, he would never be trialled for.

Nick pondered as he knew that Eileen had been put in jail but was puzzled why Conor, the other son, and Judith never stood trial. *Surely, they must have been involved*, he thought. He was free, and he and his family were alive – that was all that mattered.

It was hard not seeing his family and friends. He was now called James Taylor and resided in Keswick in the Lake District. A job was given to him sorting mail at the local post Office Depot. Nobody knew anything of Nick's past or the scale of danger he had been in. Nick still had mental scars and sleepless nights about the whole episode, and worried whether Myles could still get to him.

The house they gave him was quite modest and contemporarily styled, and he'd had a bit of input and had some pictures of his family. One of the pictures was him his Dad, his Mum and his brother sitting on some decking outside a fixed caravan in Cornwall, if he remembered correctly; what lovely memories. The safe house had a big garden with a small concrete wall. He would spend hours just kicking a ball against it, wondering what his family were doing now. His brother – was he married? Mum – was she still working at the camera shop in town? As for Dad – was he still doing his bowls and moaning about his partner's inadequacies?

Nick still recollected Myles' colourful language and ranting as he was led away from court, about to serve his jail sentence. Myles had broken free momentarily from the guards, and he had pointed and wagged his finger in the direction of three people, including Nick.

"Charles, Nick, you are marked men, dead men walking; I will have you laid the fuck out permanently. Judge, you as well!" Myles had screamed.

They'd managed to get a better grip on Myles and he was bundled out of court hastily, shortly followed by all the other members of the convicted family and associates. Nick remembered Seamus making a gun sign with his hands and pointing it at him. Luckily such retribution had not been made; it had been half a year and they didn't know where he was. He could only assume the detective had retired and most likely been given anonymity. As for the judge, they must always be getting those threats so he was probably leading a normal life, otherwise there would be no judges left with all the bad people in the world allegedly after them.

It was about 4 p.m., a breezy Autumn afternoon with the odd bit of sunshine. Next door to him a new family had moved in and he noticed they had a couple of little boys about eight and ten. The family seemed nice and had waved a few times.

A tennis ball came over the fence, and Nick thought it must be the boys'.

"Hey, mister, throw our ball back!" said the boy in an Irish accent. A year ago, that would have rung alarm bells to Nick, but it didn't nowadays.

He walked towards where the ball had landed near the back of the garden, then suddenly he heard an airplane or helicopter in the near distance.

"Get in!" an Irish lady shouted from the kitchen.

Nick saw a helicopter hovering over the field adjoining the garden. Suddenly it spun ninety degrees, the door opened and shots rained out from a machine gun.

Nick turned to run but went down like a sack of potatoes. The helicopter shut its door and rose, spun and flew off as quickly as it had appeared.

CHAPTER 39

"I have to give you some alarming news: the detective and the judge on the case have been murdered," the policeman said. He continued to give details of both hits to Nick.

"Oh my god, it's just a matter of time. You can't protect me!" Nick shouted.

"Please calm down; how are your injuries?" the policeman said, trying to lead Nick away from the info he had just learnt.

"The one that went in the hip is the worst – I can't sit, I can't stand, just can't get in a position where it doesn't hurt. I'm on every type of painkiller available. So, what are the next steps, the plans for me?" Nick said.

"Well, you have to continue on the witness protection programme at a new location," the policeman reiterated.

"To be honest, I don't hold out too much hope; there must be informants or policemen on Myles' payroll for this to happen," Nick said firmly, not too confident of the response from the officer. He was high-ranking within the policeforce and had been involved in these types of operations, but it seemed Myles had people everywhere willing to do whatever he said.

"Nick, you don't need to worry, you will be safe. At this very moment, we are putting together your new life, new identity, documents and workplace," the officer said.

"Hold on! Don't worry? *Don't worry?!* Detective Dantry was gunned down and killed, his wife left disabled from a bullet wound, and the judge was assassinated in Italy. For Christ's sake, I was nearly killed at a so-called undisclosed location safe house. I don't have the optimism you have, not one bit!" Nick said angrily.

The policeman hesitated for a few seconds then replied. "I've spoken to the doctors and they think you can go next week. So, we will move you by light aircraft to your new destination and life. I promise it will not be compromised this time. We are currently working on things so this can't happen again."

Two weeks passed and after he had done a lot of rehabilitation, the police decided Nick had to be moved as there was a chance Myles' people could locate the hospital. Late one night Nick was dressed and escorted out of the hospital under cover of darkness, and driven to an airfield. Nick boarded the plane and flew to his new destination: Wales.

In the meantime, his mother had been informed by the police of the attempted assassination on her son and that he was at a new safe house. Like Nick, she was worried as she had also learnt that the detective and judge had been successfully murdered, and it was believed to have been done by the McGinley clan.

Nick was taken to his dwelling; he entered the house and sat down with all his new documents, *déjà vu*. There were phone numbers for police departments, a mobile phone, a new driving licence, passport, bank cards and new work details. He did wonder how they could do these documents and be official. He made a quick microwave meal, then decided to go up to bed. He tossed and turned, still in much pain from the shots he took about three weeks prior. He watched a documentary about animals chasing their prey, stalking them and then finally pouncing, and it reminded him of his predicament. This in mind, he wondered when a McGinley servant would come and end his life.

CHAPTER 40

Eileen lay in her cell, condemned to fifteen years minimum until parole or a review of her case. Although her participation in the crime syndicate in any one instance had been minimal or remote, it was her knowledge of what was going on. It was hits on rival gangs, the assassination of police and judges, plus being involved in decisions on kidnapping or intimidation. In the end, all the different counts of collusion added up, and that's how the judge came to her sentence. It did not help her case that she shot and wounded a police officer.

A lady wandered into her cell. Eileen was in Holloway Prison, which was well known for holding high-category women prisoners. Despite her convictions she could get some favours for herself; friends would come to her cell; doors were opened and they'd turn a blind eye. The family's pull and influence had tentacles everywhere, including the prisons' day-to-day runnings.

"Eileen, how's your day? Beautiful weather. If only we were free, we could have a lazy day at a big country pub, sipping on Pimm's," Rosie said.

"Oh, that would be bliss, but not for a long time yet. My

close family will still be in prison or long gone. Life's over for me. I'm resigned to these four walls until about the age of fifty, minimum," Eileen said in a despondent manner.

Rosie looked at Eileen hesitantly, then went ahead with something on her mind she'd wanted to ask for months, but had never had the courage. It might stoke a heated exchange; she was about to find out.

"Eileen, I hope you don't mind me asking and I know a few inmates have asked you questions on this subject in the past, but it must have been awful being raped," Rosie said, trying to sound sincere.

Eileen glanced down at the floor for a few seconds, looked up again slowly, looked around the cell and then stared through the small window to the free world, deliberated, and then spoke.

"The rape, the rape; I've never spoken to anyone about the real truth. I've known you, Rosie, how long has it been, five or six years? You used to do some jobs for the family and now we meet up in here – life, eh!"

It seemed such a long time ago in her mind. Freedom, lots of money and all the material things she could ask for. One fateful conversation set off a chain of events.

"Rosie, it was a lie. I was never raped; I made the whole thing up. I made up a name and by some freakish coincidence there was a man or boy of that name in a nearby town. I wanted to shock and get my dad's attention; I was getting older and didn't feel like Daddy's special girl any more. I drew an innocent person into a nightmare and it nearly cost him his life. I'm just thankful he survived. All it was at that time was Seamus and Patrick – no time for me. It was boys' things, pubs and family business, which was no place for a girl, my dad thought," Eileen uttered.

"Oh, Eileen, why? It could have ended disastrously; does your father know?" Rosie enquired.

"No, he doesn't know, and apart from yourself, no one knows, so keep it that way if you know what's best," Eileen said sternly.

Rosie got the message. The friends spoke about other matters and the subject was firmly closed, never to be opened up again. Eileen asked Rosie if she wanted any treats in the jail. Rosie indicated some whisky and some cigarettes would take the sting out of the sentence. Eileen said she would sort this out and would have them to her within a week or so. Rosie was thankful to Eileen.

"Girls, enough now; Rosie back to your cell," a prison warden said.

As Rosie left the cell, she looked back at Eileen; Eileen was distant and in another world.

She snapped out of it. "Rosie, not a word," Eileen said.

Eileen gazed out of the cell window and wished she could change the sequence of events that had spiralled out of control.

Although Rosie was fearful of Eileen, she was also fearful of the threat made to her a few days before... by Conor.

Later that night, Rosie called Conor with the news he suspected. Eileen had made up the accusation against Nick Scott.

CHAPTER 41

Conor was sipping cocktails on the edge of a pool with a couple of beauties by his side at his local resort. A long way from Guildford and a better lifestyle in many ways. He had a villa in the expensive part of the Cayman Islands and had been there for about four months, and he was getting comfortable with his new surroundings and luxuries.

Every now and again he went to the resort to pick up some sorts for a party back at his place. It had now been six months since the trial, and the majority of his family had been convicted of their offences.

"Oh, babe, I've just got to make a few calls. Can you two take a little walk and get a few more drinks in; put it on my tab. Oh, and get a bottle of champagne; let's live the dream," Conor said flippantly.

He pulled out his mobile phone – it was top of the range; he loved his gadgets. At the family home in Guildford he had the latest Mac computer and one of the first mobile phones released to consumers. Rumour had it this technology had been around for years and a lot of militaries all over the world were already a couple of generations ahead of the consumer range. He dialled the number, then put the phone to his ear as it started ringing.

HMP BELMARSH

The internal phone started ringing; it rang continuously, the caller was persistent. The wardens in the office where the phone was situated looked at each other as if to say, *Who has this number? This is for outbound calls only.* It stopped momentarily but then it started again.

The senior warden moved towards the phone, picked it up and braced himself in anticipation of who it might be on the other end of the line. "Hello, HMP Belmarsh," he said authoritatively.

"Hi, I need to talk to Myles McGinley; it's his son Conor," Conor said calmly.

"I'm sorry, we don't accept incoming calls. We will ask him to call you on his next allotted time to make personal calls. How the hell have you got this number?" the warden replied.

"No, get him on the phone now," Conor insisted.

The warden thought he should, as Myles was the top guy of the prison since he had been incarcerated in Belmarsh six months ago. It was 9 p.m. and the convicts were in their cells and lights were due to be out shortly.

"Go and get Myles McGinley from 'S' wing. Take a few officers with you; make sure he's handcuffed at all times and be as quick as possible," Warden Jones said.

The other warden left the office quickly, gathered some officers *en route* and went towards S Wing. He had cuffs on him and it would take a minute or so to get there. He had been told about the notoriety of Myles since he had come to Belmarsh and was a bit apprehensive, even though the wardens were meant to be in charge.

Meanwhile, Conor spoke to the warden, a bit of small talk whilst waiting for his dad to come to the phone. He was winding the warden up, trying his patience.

"He has you dancing to his tune, does he, getting perks, I bet? You know he's a cold-blooded murderer?" Conor said.

"You can talk. You're cut from the same cloth and probably were involved in a lot of the activity," Warden Jones replied.

"No, no murdering, just electronics, bugging and hacking into computers, just for the cause. I didn't want to do it for criminal activity. I was only a political activist," Conor insisted.

The other warden reached Myles' cell and unlocked it; Myles was already dozing off.

"We don't know how but we have a call for you – it's your son Conor. He wants to talk to you now," the warden said.

After a few seconds' processing and comprehending what had been said, he chuckled and replied, "You're having a laugh. That dimwit can hardly string a sentence together; he would not have the audacity to call me. He's dyslexic and has anxiety issues; he would not make a call; it must be fake. How did he get the prison number? I didn't think it was the type of organisation that advertised in the phone directory or Yellow Pages," Myles joked.

"True, we don't know how he got it, and he's dialled an internal office number that certainly wouldn't be listed," the warden replied.

Myles contemplated for a moment. Maybe it was Conor as he was a brainbox with telephony and computer equipment and networks. Myles accompanied the officer, intrigued to hear his stuttering, stammering son on the phone and what the content might be. It would be nice to talk to his son he thought though.

Once in the office, Myles was handed the phone and he motioned the wardens away so he could try and have some privacy. He imagined Conor would be quiet and difficult to understand. "Conor, is that you?" Myles said.

"Yes, it is," Conor replied confidently, dropping the Irish accent as if he'd never had one.

"You sound different and your stammer's gone. How are you?" Myles said, surprised.

"Listen, and listen carefully. I have seized all your money, had it transferred as of midnight to me. I have notified everyone that I run the firm and everyone reports to me. No one will do or implement anything for you," Conor said firmly and arrogantly.

Myles was stunned and paused for a few moments. He could not believe what he had just heard or how Conor could have pulled this off – all his money gone in the blink of an eye. He stared at the walls in disbelief and was just about to say something when another blast of commands came down the phone from Conor.

"All the time you treated me like a nobody, I heard everything that went on. I took it in, I learnt, I bettered myself. I have a photographic memory, as you know, so I knew all the family's business. I had elocution lessons with the teacher behind your back. I educated myself during nearly every moment I wasn't playing computer games. I helped out in the finance office and got familiar with banking protocol and transactions. Added to my computer skills, I could and have lifted all your money; it's disappeared across computer land."

Myles listened in amazement and shock.

"Conor…" Myles started to say but the line went dead. Myles looked at the wardens, who'd got the basics of the conversation that had just gone on. They led Myles back towards the cell; he was in total disbelief at the conversation he had just had with his son. The warden sniggered gently, but made sure Myles didn't hear.

Meanwhile back in the Cayman Islands…

"Girls, just one more call and then I will help you polish that champagne off and inspect your bikini lines," Conor said cheekily. Conor dialled another number and waited for a reply.

Nick Scott's mobile rang. *Who knew this number?* It had been given to him by the police for the new witness programme put in place. Maybe it was someone within the police authority, or even worse, a McGinley henchman. He answered it reluctantly. "Hello?" he said tentatively.

"Hi, you don't know me; you will have a million pounds in your bank tomorrow and no one from the McGinley family will come for you. Even though I know where you are, you are of no interest to me going forward... sorry for what you and your family went through," Conor said reassuringly. The line dropped out and the call was ended.

Nick thought this could not be true, but the next day he went to the bank. He asked for a balance, and the cashier looked up at him and smiled.

"Here you go, sir, I've printed it off. I don't want to say it in front of other customers," the cashier said.

Nick took the small printout that had been folded. He unfolded it.

£1,000,567.

THE END